UNINVITED GUEST

by

Robert Rahula

ALSO BY ROBERT RAHULA

NOVELS:

Messieurs
Panamaniac
Island of Misfits
Day Another Paradise In
One Last Fling
Bathhouse Stories
Conversation in a Belgian Bar
All the Yage in Reno
Exigent Circumstances

SHORT STORIES:

Horror Stories for Children

POETRY:

Trigger Points
Dentro Del Corazón Bloqueada
Camino
Migration
I Sing the Body Politic
Wonderland
From Whose Bourn
Poemas Españoles
Expat Poems

ANTHOLOGIES:

Half Life
The Essential Dan Landes

UNINVITED GUEST
© 2018 by Robert Rahula

www.robertrahula.com

This is a work of fiction. Characters, organizations, businesses, products, locales, and events portrayed in this book either are products of the author's imagination or are used fictitiously.

First Printing, 2018
ISBN 978-0-9994736-4-1

Alma-gator Press
Barcelona • Madrid • La Chorrera

"As flies are to wanton boys..."

-William Shakespeare

Prologue

When Death—that uninvited and unwelcome guest—arrives, all plans cease; everyone has to stop and make adjustments; and everyone has to deal with it.

And so it was when Magali died. Jenny had sent one of her girls—a woman named Antonia—to drive over to Magali's apartment in Villa Rosario after Magali had failed to show up for work. Antonia knocked on Magali's door, but there was no answer. Like most of the residents of Villa Rosario, Magali didn't lock her door—there was no need in such a small town—and so, after knocking several times, Antonia opened the door and peeked inside. When she saw Magali's body crumpled on the floor, she gasped involuntarily, then ran back to her car to get her cell phone.

Chapter One

The dead are not buried under the ground in Villa Rosario. The indigenous peoples of the area consider that to be an unclean practice—a centuries-old belief that the local Catholic Church reluctantly honors in order to make itself more palatable to the locals. Nor are there any embalmers or crematoriums in Villa Rosario. As soon as the authorities release the body to the deceased's family (or, in Magali's case, to Jenny), the body is immediately wrapped in white cotton and carried that same day by sorrowful family and friends (or, in Magali's case, by sorrowful customers and lovers) to the local cemetery, where a short service is held, and the body is carefully eased into a narrow horizontal chamber in an above-ground concrete mausoleum. The door to the chamber is then sealed up with bricks and cement. When the cement dries, workers cover it with bright white stucco and embed a small sign with the deceased's name into the stucco.

Ricardo was among the mourners on this particular Saturday morning, as was Dan Landes. Both men, in their time, had each been one of Magali's many lovers, both as customers and as true lovers. As long-time friends in Villa Rosario, Ricardo and Dan were equals in each other's lives. As two of Magali's ex-lovers, they were equals in her life, and now, walking on either side of the canvas litter, helping to carry Magali's thin stiff body up the hill, they were equals in her death.

It was only ten in the morning, but already the sun was hot in the bright blue Panamanian sky. "Cielo," Ricardo mused to himself—the Spanish word for both sky and heaven, both out of reach for him, but not for Magali now. Cicadas whined a soft high shrill as Ricardo, Dan, don Fernando, and Jenny's husband Ted carried the body through the cemetery gates, followed by about twenty other mourners, including all of the girls who worked for Jenny at her brothel in the neighboring town of La Chorrera.

Ricardo, who was now seventy years old, had been worried that the effort of carrying Magali from the church up to the cemetery might be too much for him, but he was amazed how light her body was. Maybe, he thought to himself, the things that weighed her down in life had finally been lifted from her.

The four men marched slowly up to the mausoleum that Jenny had paid for, and placed the canvas litter holding Magali's body onto a wooden pallet that sat on a table directly in front of the open-mouthed concrete tomb, that horizontal slot that would be her final bed.

Jenny had asked Father Lopez to conduct the ceremony. Father Lopez was past ninety now, and had long since retired from active church life. He lived in a simple hut on the church grounds in Villa Rosario and no longer performed any church functions. But Jenny was an old friend, so he agreed to do this service. He stood by the mausoleum, swaying slightly, keeping one hand on the concrete chamber for support, and gave a short eulogy while a young altar boy in a white robe swung a brass incense holder back and forth, filling the air with the thick scent of frankincense and charcoal. Father Lopez's voice still had the authority of an old Catholic priest, but there was also an undertone of weariness.

"From ashes are we born, and to ashes we return; ashes to ashes, dust to dust; all that is not of God must die, but all that is crushed will be restored; all that is lost will be made new. For as much as it hath pleased Almighty God of His great mercy to take unto Himself the soul of our dear sister here departed, we therefore commit her body to this tomb in sure and certain hope of the Resurrection to eternal life, through our Lord Jesus Christ, who shall change our vile body, that it may be like unto His glorious body, according to the mighty working, whereby He is able to subdue all things to Himself. It is through the grace of God that we are saved, and on that final Day of Judgment, we shall join God in Heaven."

Father Lopez then nodded to don Fernando, and don Fernando turned to Ricardo, Dan and Ted, and the four men gently picked up the wooden pallet and slid Magali's body all the way inside the circular chamber of the mausoleum. Then the four men stepped back with the other mourners and watched while two workers, who had been standing nearby with bricks and a wheelbarrow half-full of cement, quickly moved into position, and sealed up the tomb's entrance with the bricks and cement. After five minutes of work, they were done, and they left, silently pushing their wheelbarrow back to their supply shed on the other side of cemetery.

Several men walked up to the mausoleum and touched it. Most of the girls—all sex workers like Magali— cried and held each other. Father Lopez gave both Jenny and Ted a hug. He said a few words to his friend don Fernando, then shook hands with Dan and Ricardo. Then he and the altar boy made their way down the footpath to the cemetery gate. Everyone else stayed by the mausoleum, crying softly, or standing silently, or talking quietly in twos and threes.

Ricardo had learned years ago that funerals are short in Central America out of necessity. In the Panamanian heat and humidity, with no embalming, bodies must be quickly sealed away. While services at the cemetery were short, there would be several weeks of long remembrances and prayer services at the local church, so that people could grieve naturally. The first one would be that night at the Catholic Church in the center of Villa Rosario, led by the regular priest. There would also be a service at the Catholic Church nearest to Jenny's brothel in La Chorrera. Attendance at the La Chorrera church would be full, as Magali had worked at Jenny's for many years, and was known—and loved—by many men in that larger city.

Ricardo walked up to Dan and asked, "Are you going to the service tonight?"

Dan shook his head no, and then asked, "You?"

Ricardo took a quick glance at the mausoleum, and said, "Maybe... I'm not sure yet." He looked at his watch and then asked Dan, "Do you want to go get a cup of coffee... or something stronger?"

"Maybe tomorrow," Dan said. "Actually, definitely tomorrow. I want to talk with you. But right now, I want to stay here until after everyone leaves and pay my final respects."

"I understand," Ricardo said. "Call me tomorrow."

"I will."

And Ricardo moved away. Ricardo understood that Dan had loved Magali too, maybe even more than he had. It was hard not to have loved Magali. There was something broken about her that needed love so much.

Ricardo said a few words to Ted and Jenny, and then he stopped and squeezed Antonia's hand. Ricardo did not visit Jenny's brothel as much these days as he used to, but he had slept with Antonia once or twice, and was fond of her. He had heard from Jenny that it was Antonia who had found Magali, and that this had been a great shock to Antonia because she and Magali were good friends.

Ricardo didn't say any words to Antonia; he just squeezed her hand and smiled. She nodded sadly, then gave him a hug.

Finally, Ricardo walked up to don Fernando, the town's police chief, and shook his hand, and then walked out of the cemetery. After a few minutes, the other guests also started making their way down the footpath, past so many other mausoleums that held their ancestors and their ancestors' ancestors, going back through the generations.

Don Fernando looked over at Dan standing solitary by Magali's mausoleum. He sensed that his friend wanted to be alone, so he left without saying goodbye.

The cicada sound in the trees seemed to drift off and stop. After a few more minutes, Dan looked around and saw he was alone. He reached into his front pocket and pulled out a small thin metal flask, lifted it discretely to his lips and drank until he had emptied it. The dark smoky pungent taste of ayahuasca slid down his throat. He recapped the flask and put it back in his pocket. Then he stepped up close to Magali's tomb and softly spoke:

"Oh Magali, I know Father Lopez meant well... but he's a priest, so what else could he say? But his words don't really give much guidance, do they? So let me tell you how it is. I know you are confused, maybe even terrified. But please, do not be afraid... You have died. Your body is dead. You have to understand this—you have to accept the fact that you have died. You are not in your body anymore. You cannot go back to your body. I know it's natural that you want to linger here near your body, but it is unnecessary... it's impossible. Your essence is no longer held in your body..."

Dan paused. He could feel the ayahuasca taking hold. There was the familiar feeling of slight nausea. He breathed deeply until it passed. Magali's mausoleum began to glow, slowly radiating a soft white light. He could feel her presence. He began to speak again:

"Ahh, there you are. Good. I know you can hear me. The thing that I'm trying to say is: Don't stay here. There's nothing here anymore."

Dan could feel the presence of other beings around him. He knew what was happening.

"I mean, look around, do you see all these ghosts? You don't want to be like them, do you?"

Dan looked around the cemetery. Hundreds of ghosts were standing there, like vibrating shadows, drawn to the light emanating from Magali's mausoleum like moths to a flame. Dan turned back to the mausoleum.

"You're going to see a lot of ghosts in the next few days, Magali. They're attracted to your light. Just ignore them. Some can be rather scary looking, but remember, they are just phantoms... images... memories... they have no power... Do you see that white light around you? That's you. That's what you are now, just that light. Try and let yourself dissolve into it. That's all you have to do.

Dan paused again. The light from the mausoleum was pulsating now. The earth was humming. Ayahuasca was whispering in his ear that it was time to go.

"I have to go now, Magali. I just had to feel you one more time... to say goodbye... and to tell you to not be afraid. You're not the first person to die. Everyone goes through this. Don't hang around here. Just let yourself move forward."

He choked up on the last word. He knew what he had said was true, but he didn't know where "forward" led to. He took a breath and turned and walked through the shadows of other creatures gathering around Magali's tomb. As he made his way down the footpath, the cicadas in the trees started their song again.

Chapter Two

It was Dan's voice that gave Magali the incentive to move. She had been listening so carefully to everyone's voice, everyone's inner thoughts, but it was Dan's words that finally made her realize where she was, hugging so tightly to her own body. She lifted her head and looked down. It was odd—she could see perfectly well even in the pitch-black enclosure. She could see her blue-gray face through the cotton wrapping. Dan was right—she was dead. She unloosened her arms from around the body and began to move, to expand.

At first she was afraid that she could not leave the mausoleum. But she quickly realized that the walls were porous, soft and spongy, with thousands of holes. She flowed slowly out through the walls. There was Dan, leaning against the mausoleum. She flowed around him, sensing him, feeling the memory of his body. Other lights seemed to be moving in towards them. She looked at them. They were pulsating light, too. But they moved in shadowy bodies. How did they get bodies? Were these the ghosts that Dan was talking about? Dan looked like he was about to cry. She wanted to pat his head and say, "There, there, nothing to cry about."

She watched as Dan walked slowly out of the cemetery. She decided that she would go visit him later, to tell him that everything was okay. She looked over at all the other shadows moving closer to her. Yes, she would go visit everyone, and tell them that everything was okay. But first she wanted to talk with these shadows.

Chapter Three

Father Lopez had walked back down the hill to the Church, to the changing room behind the Sanctuary. He removed his funeral vestments and hung them in the priests' closet. He did not like doing services any more—they wore him out—and the changing room smelled mustier than the old days. The smell reminded him of how old and heavy the Church had become... but Jenny had asked him to lead the procession and to conduct the service, and so he had agreed... as a favor to Jenny... well, to be honest, he agreed because of his memory of Magali and the kindness she had once shown him.

He slipped his old clothes on—simple heavy white cotton pants and a shirt—and walked slowly out the back door and across the small patio to his cottage. This was the old priest's residence, the "retirement house" the Church called it, but it was where the old priests like him were relegated to spend their last years, i.e., where old priests like him went to die. He remembered some sixty years earlier, when he had been ordained as the Parish Priest of this Church, how Father Veteto had moved from the spacious priest's apartment on the other side of the Church into this small cottage, and how he complained about the dank cramped quarters. Back then, it was inconceivable to Father Lopez that he would follow in Father Veteto's footsteps— that he would stay the parish priest in Villa Rosario for so many decades, never advancing further... that he would age and shrivel... and that he would also end up in this hut. Father Veteto had only lasted two years in this cottage before he died of pneumonia. So far, Father Lopez had outlasted him by a decade. Of course, Father Lopez had the advantage of electricity. He had made the Church run an electric line to the cottage before he moved in at age seventy-nine. That way, he had a small heater he could turn on when the nights got too cold and damp, and a small refrigerator and hot plate for food. Father Lopez had been convinced that it was the dampness that had killed Father Veteto, and he didn't want to go that way—coughing himself to death night after night.

He opened the door of the cottage and stepped inside. Even though the sun was high and bright in the sky, the inside of his cottage was still cool. The thick concrete walls always kept it cool. He left the front door open, to let some warmth and light in, and he walked over to the sink and pulled a bottle out from beneath and got a glass from the cupboard and poured himself a glass of wine, and went to sit down in the large easy chair in the corner.

An excess of wine was the one sin he allowed himself these days... well no, that wasn't true. His life had been one long string of sins, he thought, but certainly no worse than other priests—in fact, probably less sin than other priests. He had served his congregation without scandal, and had performed many services to protect them over the decades, such as working in secret with don Fernando to drive the brujos out of town. In fact, many of the services he had performed were quite secret. He remembered meeting Magali when she was just fourteen years old and pregnant by her uncle.

He sipped at his wine and let his mind think back to Magali. He didn't hear the rustle of leaves outside. He didn't notice the almost imperceptible light that had moved into the room and was now surrounding him. Poor Magali, he thought to himself, what a sad doomed life.

It wasn't that long ago, he thought, not really... no more than, what? Fifteen or sixteen years? Just a drop in the bucket, really. He remembered Magali's mother coming to him sobbing hysterically. He remembered how confused Magali was. The congregation only knew that her uncle disappeared suddenly one day and never returned to Villa Rosario. But Father Lopez knew... he knew all the secrets of his parishioners. After all, he heard all their confessions, so he knew where the uncle's body was buried.

The hardest thing about being a parish priest—he had learned—had nothing to do with his faith in God... it was maintaining his faith in people... after listening month after month, and year after year, to the unspeakable things they did to each other... Is there any worse job in the world than to sit for decades in that dark confession box and hear of the infidelities, the murders, the rapes, the betrayals, the lies, the frauds, the crimes, the continual unspeakable horrors that his flock of faithful peasants inflicted upon each other and upon themselves? There were times when he thought that the job of priest must have been designed by the Devil. Sworn to confessional secrecy by the Church, he could do nothing but listen and endure, and let those horrible confessions seep through his church robes and blacken his soul. No wonder God gave us the story of Job, he thought. It was a story meant for priests. There were times when he'd climb to the pulpit and look out at his parish and see all those shiny faces looking up to him for hope and guidance and words of Christian love and forgiveness, and he'd see only darkened wretched souls who never stopped sinning, who would do the penances he gave them but then slip away that same night to sleep with a neighbor's wife or cheat a friend. The sinning never stopped.

But then, was he any better?

He took another sip of wine and thought again about Magali, about that night when her sobbing mother brought that frightened girl to see him. Fourteen and pregnant, and trembling with that black eye where her father had beaten her for being pregnant... as if it was her fault. A family that couldn't afford the children they had, much less another one, much less the public shame that would follow them... and follow her...

It was a time when he was nearing retirement, that night fifteen years ago... He had walked for decades amongst murderers, thieves, adulterers... all the criminals of Villa Rosario—why, he knew them better than don Fernando did, and don Fernando had been their police chief for almost twenty years! And he knew the shame that would follow Magali if people knew she was with child, and how his parishioners would shun her family, and so when Magali's mother asked him for guidance, he knelt with her and told her to pray that God would intervene, and then afterwards he told her to come back that night with Magali and that he would give them a special communion... and so he did—a private communion service that night right there in the Church, where Magali and her mother knelt at the railing, and he gave them the wafer representing the body of Christ and the wine representing the blood of Christ... except for Magali, he substituted grape juice, as was the custom for children, except that this goblet of grape juice had a dose of Misoprostol in it, and he held the goblet so that Magali had to drink it all.

The next day, Magali's mother came by the Church to tell Father Lopez that her prayers had been answered, and that Magali had spontaneously aborted the pregnancy that night. Father Lopez nodded and commented that God moves in mysterious ways, and that it would probably be best if the family kept this miracle to themselves and just attended Mass more often. It was a few days later that Magali's father came to him and confessed that he had killed Magali's uncle—his wife's brother—when he had discovered what had happened. Father Lopez hadn't anticipated that, but... all in all... he thought it resolved the matter, so he gave Magali's father the same advice—that it would be best for Magali and the family to keep that secret to himself and to come to Mass more often, and maybe do some volunteer work around the Church.

Father Lopez had gotten the Misoprostol from Jenny. She had told him how much to mix into the grape juice. He hadn't thought about these things in a long time. He didn't regret what he had done, but he did wonder, as the years went by, whether it had made any difference. Magali had ended up working as a prostitute for Jenny's brothel over in La Chorrera. And while Jenny was a good friend and ran a safe clean brothel, he always wondered if Magali's life would have turned out any worse if she had had that baby... assuming of course, she could have survived childbirth at home, which is where it would have happened, as Villa Rosario did not have a hospital.

He got up and refilled his glass and sat back down in his easy chair. When did his soul get so black? Thank God he had his wine. Thank God he was nearing the end of life.

He took another sip and thought of Jenny. It was funny, he thought, that the same men in his congregation who would condemn and shun young girls like Magali who happened to get pregnant, saw no problem with slipping away to Jenny's brothel whenever they got a few extra dollars in their pocket. Ahh, Jenny, he thought. What a complex woman. She could walk down the streets of La Chorrera or Villa Rosario and no one would say a word against her—not even behind her back. How did she do it? Was it that she simply refused to acknowledge that there was any problem with what she did? Was it that she simply treated the whoring business like any other service that the community needed? Or was it the Panamanian culture where wives just accepted their husbands would cheat and were glad that Jenny ran a clean brothel where there was no risk of disease? Or was it just her personality? Father Lopez didn't know. But there was certainly something about her that placed her on a higher plane than other people.

The light swirled around Father Lopez's feet and floated up behind him. He thought of the few times that

Jenny came to church. It was only on special occasions, such as weddings or, like today, for funerals. She would always come with her husband Ted. Now there was a strange marriage, Father Lopez thought. Ted, a gringo, lived in Villa Rosario, where he owned and managed a small apartment complex. Jenny lived in La Chorrera in her own place near her brothel. Yet they had been happily married for almost thirty years. And they always appeared so loving whenever he saw them together. Maybe that was the secret to a good marriage, Father Lopez thought—keeping separate houses.

The light behind him began to swirl, but Father Lopez was deep in thought. Sometimes Jenny's girls would come to Mass... never to the early Mass, of course... They always sat together quietly in the back. If any of the men recognized them, they never said anything, lest they themselves be unmasked by their comments. No, they would just bow their heads and pray more earnestly than usual.

Father Lopez remembered when Magali became one of Jenny's workers. Jenny had brought it up one day when she and Father Lopez were visiting together in La Chorrera. She had just announced it as a fact: "You remember Magali from your village? She wants to come and work for me."

Father Lopez wasn't sure if Jenny was asking permission or simply sharing something that had already been decided. He tried to read Jenny's expression, but it told him nothing. "Oh?" he finally replied, not knowing what else to say.

"Yes," Jenny said. "She actually approached me two years ago, but I said no. I didn't want to tell her that her father was a customer. But then he passed away a few months ago, and so when she approached me last week, I told her yes."

Father Lopez just nodded. Jenny didn't need to explain more. Magali's father had worked in a sugar cane mill outside of Villa Rosario, and between the cutting machines and the presses, industrial accidents at the mill were common. Without his wages, Magali's mother would not be able to pay bills or care for Magali's six younger brothers and sisters. It was a common story in Panama. In poor families, if the eldest daughter did not marry money, she often became a prostitute.

Cane farming and prostitution—the two oldest professions, Father Lopez thought.

He took another sip of wine and let himself sink deeper into memory. The light around him continued to swirl and pulsate.

Chapter Four

Jenny had driven back to La Chorrera. She had dropped off Antonia and two other girls at their apartments and then drove over to the brothel and parked in the garage. She owned the building. She had bought it decades ago with the money she had saved working as a prostitute in Panama City—money she had scraped and fought for because she knew that her productive years as a hooker were limited. Income for a sex worker is totally dependent on either beauty or brains, and Jenny had both, and she was smart enough to know, even back then, that beauty fades very quickly. It's not the sex that takes its toll on the body—it's the long hours, all night long, every night. Humans evolved to sleep at night, and anyone who works night—at any job—ages faster.

The brothel was an elegant three-story house on a quiet street in La Chorrera. It sat there without sign, red lights or any fanfare. A large tree shaded the cement walkway that led up to the front door. Inside the front door was a large parlor where Jenny would vet the clients. Upstairs were six small bedrooms, each with its own bathroom and shower.

Jenny went into the kitchen in the back of the brothel and made a pot of tea. She hadn't had lunch, but she wasn't particularly hungry. She sat down at the kitchen table while her tea was steeping and thought about whether she wanted to open the brothel tonight or not. She knew that the regular clients would have read Magali's obituary in the paper or heard about it on the street and wouldn't be coming by tonight, anyway. So in all probability, she wouldn't be losing that much money. Plus she knew that none of the girls who knew Magali would feel like working. So Jenny decided to give the girls the night off. She would text them all, and post a small sign on the door. To be honest, Jenny thought to herself, she didn't feel like working tonight, either. She was getting too old for this business, night after night. Maybe it was time to think about retiring… She got out her cell phone and sent a group text to her girls. Then she dug out a small 3x5 card from one of the drawers and wrote "Closed Due to Death in Family" and went and taped it to the front door.

She walked back into the kitchen and checked on her tea—it looked ready. She added a lump of sugar and took it over to the kitchen table and sat back down. She sat there sipping on the tea and thinking about Magali.

A soft light filled the hallway. It was warm and flowed through the room, softly illuminating everything, and moved towards Jenny.

What was it about Magali, Jenny wondered, that made her so special? Jenny had always been impersonal about the whoring business—it was just a business— and all her girls over the years were as fungible and interchangeable as all the clients. It had always been that way. Jenny had always been "all business", and yet… and yet… she had always treated Magali differently… what was it about Magali? Was it that she reminded Jenny of herself—her innocent self—before she had moved to Panama City and became a whore? There was something—or someone—so lost about Magali. Jenny remembered the day, so many years ago, that Magali first came to her and asked to work there. Jenny had turned her down—she was too young, too innocent. Jenny had seen too many young girls who thought they could become prostitutes and not have the business turn them bitter. Those girls were always wrong. They always assumed that just because they had fucked boys in high school so that the boys would keep them as their girlfriends, that fucking strangers for money was no different. But it *was* different, and fucking three or four men a night, night after night, hardens a woman, makes a woman view all men as simply horny bulls that had to be stroked to disgorge their semen as fast as possible; it makes a woman view all transactions as barter, all the world as one big trick to turn. Whoring hardens women because those attitudes were unavoidably realistic and obvious—all men *are* simply horny bulls, and all transactions are barter, and the whole wide world is one big trick to turn... and if you don't turn that trick, the whore in the next room will, and *she'll* make the money... yes, whoring hardens women, makes them as calculating as men... and yet, it hadn't hardened Magali. Maybe that was it, Jenny thought, maybe it was the fact that even after years of working at the brothel, Magali still seemed as innocent as the day she came knocking at Jenny's door looking for work.

The light around Jenny pulsated and moved in closer, wrapping Jenny in a translucent glow. Jenny didn't notice the light, but she suddenly felt so sad for Magali. Maybe she should have turned Magali down, not hired her that second time she came asking for work... after all, she had turned her down the first time for exactly that reason—that Magali was too innocent for whoring—but after Magali's father had died, and she came back looking for work... well... Jenny knew how bad off Magali's mom and sisters were... so she let Magali join the brothel, and taught her how to whore— how to inspect a man's private parts without insulting him, how to coax him into taking a shower before sex, how to insist on condoms no matter how a man pleaded, how to charge for extra services, how to touch a man so he came faster, how to convince a man he was the best lover ever... all the tricks of the trade that drain all the sentiment and illusion out of sex, all the techniques make the sex act no different than taking a shit before the next meal... yes, she had taught Magali all those tricks, and yet... somehow, there was still an innocence to Magali that made Jenny worry about her.

After Magali had worked there a year, Jenny noticed that Ricardo always asked for her when he came to the brothel, and she noticed that Magali seemed to like him as well. So when Magali left the brothel work to live with Ricardo, Jenny really hoped it would lead to marriage. Yes, Ricardo was older, but that was good. After all, Ted was older and he and Jenny had a good marriage. With certain men, older can mean wiser. Jenny approved of Ricardo, and encouraged Magali to try and make that relationship work.

But it hadn't worked. They lived together for several months in Ricardo's apartment in Villa Rosario, but Magali eventually came back to work for Jenny. Jenny didn't understand why Magali had left Ricardo. The only thing that Magali had told Jenny was that she had wanted to fall in love with Ricardo, but somehow love never showed up. Magali had described it as standing on the cliff of love waiting for fate to push her over, but that push never came. Jenny had tried to tell her that love made no difference—that Ricardo was a good man and she should go back to him. But Magali was stubborn. She said she had to be in love to get married. That poor, poor deluded girl, Jenny thought. Stupid love stars in her eyes... of all the reasons to get married, love was the worst reason.

Years later, of course, love did find Magali. Jenny remembered when Magali confided that she thought she was falling in love with Dan. Jenny didn't think that it would work out—and it didn't. Jenny liked Dan, but simply thought he was wrong for Magali—he was too selfish, too wrapped up in himself to take on someone who needed as much attention as Magali. Ricardo would have been the better choice... but that was always the problem with love—it makes bad choices.

Jenny finished her cup of tea and looked around the room. She would miss this place if she sold the house, but maybe it was time to think about retiring. She was financially secure. Ted had talked recently about selling his small apartment building in Villa Rosario. If he sold the apartment building and she sold the brothel, they would be very well-off. Maybe it was time to make the move. They were both getting older now. Who knew how much time they had left? Magali's dying so young made that point all the more clear. Who knows how much time is allotted to us here on earth?

The light around Jenny moved from the kitchen through the downstairs parlor, up the stairs, and slowly through each room.

Chapter Five

It was nighttime now. Ricardo was fast asleep when Magali entered his dreaming. He was walking in a train station, and the trains were coming and going. Everyone was speaking a language he couldn't understand. He didn't know where he was. He looked at one train and saw Magali staring at him through a window. The train was pulling out.

Magali knew this was Ricardo's dream and that he was just supposed to get a glimpse of her as the train was leaving, but she decided to ignore his dream plan. She got up from her seat and ran down the aisle to the door and jumped off the train steps as the train was pulling out. She landed on the wooden platform.

Moving through Ricardo's dream was different than moving from the cemetery down the hill to Father Lopez's cottage—she was floating, except that her form looked like she was walking... and her form looked crisp... defined. She still felt shadowy, like smoke, but she had the appearance of a body. She stood up on her tiptoes on the platform and looked through the crowd for Ricardo. There he was, still staring at the train. She ran up to him and grabbed his arm. He looked at her in surprise.

"Don't worry," she said to him. "I'm only here for a few minutes. Then I'll leave and you can sleep." She almost had to yell to be heard over the noise of the trains pulling in and out of the station.

"Come on," she said, pulling him along. "Let's go somewhere quieter."

Ricardo gave in and let her lead him through the

crowd. There were so many people, but she pulled him to a small bench against a wall that had a corner wall that buffered the sound. She made him sit down and started talking to him.

"You know I've died," she said. "I was in the tomb at the cemetery and I heard Dan explaining to me that I had died. I'm going to go see him later tonight and talk to him. I don't think I was supposed to die this early, but I know I'm dead. If you see him, tell him you saw me. But I wanted to come see you first."

To Ricardo, everything Magali was saying made no sense. It was like two dreams colliding. This was supposed to be a train station, not a dream about real life events. The sides of his dream, where the trains were coming in and out of the station, began to rip, like a moving picture screen being torn in two. Behind it was another movie playing. It was the memory of the cemetery that morning, the bright sun in the blue sky. He was walking up the hill, helping to carry the canvas litter that held Magali's body. "Cielo" he thought, the Spanish word for both sky and heaven...

Ricardo awoke abruptly, feeling very disturbed. The image in his mind was so vivid—him sitting on the bench in the train station talking to Magali and the entire view of the trains behind him ripping in half like a rear-projection movie screen being cut down the middle. He got up and went to his writing table and started writing down everything that happened in the dream: the train station, seeing Magali, her grabbing his arm, what she said to him.... He wanted to remember it all.

Chapter Six

Later that night, way after midnight, Dan woke up. He had managed to pass out in his own bed—as he usually did when he drank ayahuasca—but now the effect of the drug was wearing off. He felt groggy, his mouth was dry, his head hurt, and the slight nausea was back. He looked at the clock—almost three. He reached over to his nightstand where he kept a bottle of water and took a long drink. That helped his dryness, but he still felt bleary. He put the bottle back on the table and stared at the dark ceiling and thought about Magali. He had loved her, but like all the other men in life, he had only loved her part-time. He envied Ricardo—at least Ricardo had tried to live with her. Of course, that was years before he and Magali had become lovers. Dan had once asked Ricardo why it hadn't worked out with Magali. Ricardo had just said, "She was just too damaged." At the time, Dan thought Ricardo was crazy to say that... but a few years later, when Dan started loving her, he finally understood.

Magali was the kind of woman who appeared to have it all together. Maybe that's something women learn to do to survive in a man's world... but she had everyone convinced. It wasn't that she was just smart, pretty, organized, and sexy—it was that she always had an answer, and her answers were always rational and convincing. Maybe that's why Dan couldn't see the damage that Ricardo had referred to—because Magali covered it so well. But... like all make-up, eventually it smeared. He remembered that one night, so many years ago now, when he first saw a glimmer of the chaos that churned beneath her carefully-controlled façade, when he first realized that Ricardo had been right...

He reached over to the nightstand to grab the bottle of water for another sip when he heard her voice.

"Thinking about me?"

Even before he turned and looked, Dan's first thought was that the ayahuasca was obviously still coursing through his system. So it did not surprise him when he turned and saw Magali sitting in the chair across from his bed. She looked as pretty and vibrant as when she was alive.

"I was," he said calmly. Dan knew visions were normal with ayahuasca—after all, that's why he used it. The visions gave him power, gave him the ability to see past the normal, to see spirits. They came to him and told him truths. So of course, this was another ayahuasca vision. The trick was not to look at it too long... to just take short glances at it and look away. That kept it under control.

"I came by to thank you," she said, "for what you said at the cemetery. I hadn't realized I was dead."

But it was hard not to look at Magali, because she was so beautiful, and he had once loved her. He started to feel sad, so he made himself look away again. He looked over at the clock. That's when his rational mind started to cut through his grogginess. He started calculating. His rational mind told him that the ayahuasca should be almost out of his system by now—he shouldn't be seeing visions this long after drinking it. Something was wrong. He looked back at the chair. She was still sitting there.

"Well," he stammered, "no one ever does, not at first."

"How did you know that?" she asked.

"I've talked to a lot of... a lot of dead people... spirits, you know. They all tell me the same thing—that when you die, you don't realize you're dead at first."

Dan looked back at the clock, recalculated the hours again in his head since he had drank the ayahuasca, then pulled himself up to a sitting position in the bed. Even though he felt like his rational mind was fully functional, his head still hurt; so this *had* to be the effect of the ayahuasca. He willed himself to treat this as a vision—there was no other option. He looked at his hands, then back at the chair where Magali was still sitting.

"Don't worry," she said, "I'm going to leave in a minute, and you can go back to sleep. I have other people I want to see. But I'll come back to talk with you after you and Ricardo talk."

Dan looked around the room. Everything was normal except that Magali was sitting there. He was fully awake now and remembering things he had learned from other ayahuasca journeys. He suddenly realized what was wrong—Magali shouldn't be appearing as a body!

"Wait a minute," he exclaimed. "How did you get a form? You're not supposed to do that! You don't want to be a ghost! You'll be trapped here!"

Magali laughed, "You always did worry too much about me." And then she simply disappeared.

"Fuck!" he yelled, and jumped out of bed. "Magali! Come back! Goddamnit!"

But she was gone.

Chapter Seven

It was almost dawn. Antonia was asleep in her bed. Magali didn't want to disturb her, didn't want to enter her dreaming, but she did want to feel Antonia's body one more time. Magali flowed through the room, over to Antonia's bed, and let herself float over the bed. Then she lowered herself down, sinking through the covers... through Antonia's nightshirt... down onto Antonia's naked body. Magali wrapped her light around Antonia's flesh, around that lithe body, spreading out over that warm cinnamon-colored skin, those soft supple breasts, the boy-like hips, the soft hair between her legs, those long lissome legs. Magali let her light move in time with Antonia's breathing: in and out, in and out. And for the briefest of moments, Magali felt the stirring of the emotion that she remembered as human sadness—that longing to touch something forever lost, to feel that feeling of flesh touching flesh, now forever gone...

Antonia had been more than Magali's best friend at the brothel—she and Magali had been lovers. They used to meet at Antonia's apartment after work several times a week because Antonia had the bigger and better shower. There they would shower together, using large sponges to "wash off the work" as they laughingly called scrubbing each other's bodies. They would both douche with a mild mixture of vinegar and water to wash out any remaining lubricant that coated the condoms they had made the men wear. All the girls who worked at the brothel hated the taste of lubricant. Jenny bought all different kinds of condoms for the girls, some with flavored lubricant, some claiming to use flavorless lubricant—but it was no use—there was no way to avoid that taste of lubricant. Jenny insisted that the girls all make the men wear condoms for all sex, and that included oral sex. And since all men want oral sex, there was no way for the girls to avoid putting their lips around condom-covered cocks. And no matter what flavors (or lack of flavors) the condom manufacturers came up with, there was always that slight machine oil taste to condoms.

Most of the girls who came to work at the brothel—if they weren't lesbian when they started—soon adopted a Sapphic lifestyle. After that much sex with those animals called men, who wouldn't prefer women? No matter if they made the men shower before sex, they were still men: men with hairy backs, men with protruding guts, men with scratchy beards, men with ugly tattoos, ugly faces, ugly leering smiles, ugly personalities... and so many ugly cocks... short fat cocks, twisted and bent cocks, tiny cocks, thin cocks with huge heads like weird mushrooms... and of course, the worst thing of all was that the girls had no say-so in selecting the men.

At least Jenny didn't let the men choose the girls. Jenny's brothel was unique in Panama that way—Jenny would meet any new customer at the door and take them into the parlor and chit-chat with them, making idle conversation at first, and then deftly asking them about their likes and dislikes. This way Jenny could weed out any police, drunks, druggies or crazies... and then Jenny would select the girl she thought was most appropriate for the man and use the in-house phone system to call that girl downstairs. If the man didn't like the girl's appearance, there was no second choice—the man had to leave. But if the man was satisfied with the girl's appearance, and they usually were, then the girl would take the man upstairs and discuss price. The girls appreciated this method because it provided some protection to them against creeps and crazies—but Jenny really did it to protect herself. Although prostitution was legal in Panama, running a brothel was not. But this way, Jenny never touched the money, she simply "introduced" men to some of her friends. Of course, the girls would bring the money to Jenny afterwards and Jenny would count it out and give the girls their share. But all in all it was a good arrangement, and since Jenny had the prettiest whores in La Chorrera working for her, the men complied with her methodology.

And Jenny always insisted on safe sex, no matter what. No amount of money was worth dying for, she often told the girls. So Jenny provided all the condoms and different types of lubricants. And the girls all used them... which led to the after-work problem, when some of the girls, like Magali and Antonia, got together. The last thing they wanted was to taste that same lubricant again that night. Nothing spoiled good lesbian sex than for a girl to go down between her lover's legs and taste that nasty lubricant in her lover's pussy.

Truth be told, it's not that Magali and Antonia made love that often. Like most of the lesbian couples who worked at Jenny's, most of the time they would just lie in each other's arms and kiss. That was an activity that all the customers at Jenny's—or any other brothel—knew: that kissing was off-limits. Even after servicing four or five men in a night, the girls would not have done any kissing. So, to come over to Antonia's apartment afterwards, to shower and then slide into bed next to Antonia's lithe body, and just hold each other, and kiss each other for thirty or forty minutes before falling asleep together, was a sex act more intimate, more personal, more connected than the hours of pounding fucking that they both had just endured.

And so it was tonight as Magali's light wrapped itself around Antonia's body... Magali just wanted to feel that connection again, one last time, that feeling of safety that comes from lying in a lover's arms... and maybe that's why the feeling that Magali remembered as human sadness came back... because what used to make that feeling of safety so comforting, so real, is that Antonia would wrap her arms around Magali too, and hold Magali close... and that feeling, that response, that type of human activity... was now lost to Magali forever.

Magali let her light loosen from around Antonia, let herself float up over the bed and out through the walls of Antonia's apartment.

Chapter Eight

Dan woke up around noon the next day. His head hurt, but he could tell the ayahuasca was completely out of his system. Still, he took a quick glance at the chair across from his bed to make sure it was empty.

It was.

He got up and went into the bathroom to piss. Then he returned to his bed and laid back down and just thought about Magali's visit the night before... assuming, of course, that it was Magali he had seen. He wasn't sure what to think, so he held both options open in his mind. Either he had brewed the ayahuasca a bit stronger than normal and what he saw last night was simply a vision... or... he actually had a conversation with Magali's spirit. Both were equally possible. Ever since he had become an ayahuasca *devoto* five years ago, he had seen many strange things—and this would not be the first time he had talked to spirits who seemed to be flesh-and-blood real. But this was different, he realized— because he had loved Magali when she was alive and he still had feelings for her now. But to give in to love with a spirit was a whole other thing. Spirits could be good guides; but when it comes to love, they cannot be trusted. You fall in love with a spirit, and they with you, and then they can turn you into a spirit too. Not a good business.

He reached over to his nightstand and picked up his cell phone and texted Ricardo to see if Ricardo wanted to meet at the Taqueria la Esquinita for lunch (or, in Dan's case, for breakfast). While he waited for a response, he thought more about Magali. What he had told her last night was true—that over the years he *had* talked to other spirits, and they all had told him that when they first died, they just didn't realize they were dead. But, Dan thought, the same was true for the living… when someone we love dies, we can't grasp it at first, either. What he had told Magali in the cemetery was also important advice for him—he had to realize that she was dead. *He* had to let go of her, too.

His cell phone beeped. Ricardo had texted back saying that he could meet him at the restaurant in about an hour. Good, Dan thought. That would give him time to shower. He got back out of bed, went into the kitchen and got the coffee pot going, and then went into the bathroom to shower.

While he was lathering up and washing himself, he thought about how strange flesh was. It was soft, flexible, pleasurable, but ultimately, temporary… like clothes that are discarded once they wear out. But spirit, on the other hand, spirit was vaporous, without form or sensation, yet ultimately… permanent. What a weird paradox, he thought to himself. No wonder people want to believe in reincarnation or resurrection or some kind of transformation back into flesh. He washed his hair and wondered if spirits maybe grew old and died, too… and if so, where does a spirit go after it dies?

He turned off the water, grabbed a towel to dry himself and thought of Father Lopez, who had looked so frail standing there beside Magali's mausoleum. He had gotten to know Father Lopez because of his friendship with don Fernando. Don Fernando and Father Lopez had been lifelong friends, and had worked together as a team in the political world of the town. Like most other towns in Panama, Villa Rosario had an elected mayor and city council; but it was really don Fernando, as the town's police chief, who had run the city for so many decades, telling the different elected mayors who to appoint to what position, which city projects to approve and which to deny. . But don Fernando never made a move without consulting Father Lopez because, after all, it was Father Lopez who knew all the secrets of the town. Don Fernando had told Dan how, one time decades ago, a certain rich man from Panama City wanted to open a fancy restaurant in Villa Rosario, and presented a very appealing proposal to the city council. But Father Lopez knew from the confessions of his parishioners that this man was just a front for drug dealers in Panama City who wanted to use the restaurant to launder money and to sell drugs in Villa Rosario. Father Lopez told don Fernando, and don Fernando went to the mayor, and for some unknown reason, the man could never obtain the city's approval to build his restaurant. Every revised plan the man submitted was stonewalled or rejected. Teams of lawyers came to Villa Rosario to argue on behalf of the man, but it was to no avail. The gringos in town, who tended to spend most of their time in restaurants, all complained that there was too much red tape in Villa Rosario and that was why it was such a backwards village. But gringos, of course, couldn't vote, and the local villagers never protested. If the city council didn't want the restaurant, there must be a good reason. And besides, the locals couldn't afford to go a fancy restaurant anyway, so it was no loss to them. Eventually the rich man from Panama City gave up on Villa Rosario and went to Villa Belén, northwest of Panama City, and opened his restaurant there. A few years later, the restaurant was busted for being a drug distribution center.

Dan poured himself a cup of coffee and sipped on it while he got dressed, and continued thinking about Father Lopez and don Fernando, and about the political team they had been for so many years—the perfect union of church and state. Of course, after Father Lopez retired and was no longer dipping into the informational spring waters of the town and sharing that knowledge with don Fernando... well, don Fernando's grip on the town's politics and future began to lessen. The town had grown, and more gringos were moving there. The city even let a consortium of investors build the town's first condominium project up in the hills overlooking Villa Rosario. But modernization brings money, and money brings corruption. Drugs eventually found their way into Villa Rosario along with WiFi, YouTube, Facebook and all the rest of mankind's penchants for wasting time. In the past, don Fernando's skill as police chief had been based on his ability to prevent crime by knowing who was who in town and what everyone was up to. But without Father Lopez's advice, as the town grew, crime began to slowly creep into Villa Rosario. And crime investigation was not don Fernando's forte—he was an old school police chief. So, over the past few years, don Fernando had dragged Dan into cases where some type of criminal investigation was necessary. After all, criminal investigation *was* Dan's forte— he had spent too many years as a detective in Los Angeles. And don Fernando knew this. And even though Dan had retired to Panama to leave that world behind, don Fernando had become his friend; and he couldn't turn his friend down when don Fernando asked for help. And that was happening more and more often.

Even with Magali, don Fernando had called Dan even before his men had removed her body from her apartment. Dan first assumed that don Fernando was doing him a kindness—calling him first so that Dan didn't hear it on the street—but after listening to don Fernando describe the state of Magali's apartment in depth, Dan realized that don Fernando had not called out of kindness, but rather to use him as an investigative sounding board. So Dan had turned on his "cop brain," clamped down on his feelings, and listened to don Fernando tell him about Magali's apartment.

The police had found a line of white powder, a razor blade, a spoon and a half-full syringe on the table near where Magali's body was found. Overdoses were no longer unusual in Villa Rosario, but this one had surprised don Fernando. He knew that Jenny strictly forbade her girls to use drugs. He knew that Jenny could spot a drug user a mile away and would have fired Magali immediately, even on just the suspicion that Magali was high. So finding drugs and a syringe on the table next to Magali's dead body made no sense to don Fernando. He checked Magali's arms. There were no signs of needle tracks.

That was when he had called Dan.

When don Fernando told him about the white powder and syringe, Dan was surprised but not shocked. He knew that Magali liked to drink. It was one of the things they used to do together, one of the things they had in common. She could drink to excess, and often did. She used to call it "reaching for the numb button". It was one of the worries he had about her when they broke up—that she would move from drinking to drugs and get in over her head. So many prostitutes used drugs to blot out the sex, to make it through another night of being fucked by strangers. But Dan agreed with don Fernando that Jenny would have spotted it. Still, when don Fernando was telling him these things, Dan's "cop brain" stayed on. The fact that there were no needle marks on her arm could easily be explained by her wanting to avoid being caught by Jenny. Drugs can be injected anywhere in the body. Dan remembered one druggie back in L.A. who used to inject heroin under her tongue to avoid track marks. Dan told don Fernando it was too early to jump to conclusions—that he just needed to send the syringe and the white powder to the police laboratory in Panama City. While Villa Rosario did not have a hospital, it did have an ambulance service with nurses. So he told don Fernando to have one of the nurses get a sample of Magali's blood and send that to the laboratory as well. If the blood sample came back with drugs that matched the drugs in syringe or on the table, then the conclusion would be obvious.

Don Fernando agreed with Dan and thanked him for the advice. Then, as an afterthought he said, "I am sorry, Dani."

"Yeah, me too," Dan said, and hung up.

That evening, Jenny called Dan and explained that the police were going to release Magali's body to her, and asked if Dan would agree to be one of the pallbearers for the funeral the next morning.

"Of course," Dan said.

Jenny went on to say that she was going to ask Father Lopez to conduct a brief service at the cemetery because of Father Lopez's special relationship to Magali. Dan didn't know that Father Lopez knew Magali, but he liked the old priest, so he told Jenny that was a good idea.

After he hung up the phone from talking to Jenny, he realized that he had been clamping down on his feelings all day since don Fernando's call. That's when he decided to prepare a small mixture of ayahuasca in a flask to take to the cemetery for the funeral. He knew that he would need it. As hardened as he was, he knew he had to talk with her one more time, had to feel her presence one more time... and ayahuasca was the only way to do that. And he was right—it was the only way he had gotten through the day yesterday.

He finished getting dressed and refilled his coffee cup. He thought again of Father Lopez. Yes, Father Lopez had looked frail at the cemetery. Dan made a mental note to go and talk with him. The old priest might not be around for much longer.

The thought of Father Lopez dying seemed to awaken the sadness he felt about Magali. It wasn't just sadness; it was more of a conflicted feeling, and it made him feel weak. He took a deep breath and pushed the feeling down by reminding himself that he really hadn't seen much of Magali in the past two years anyway—that it wasn't that death had taken her out of his life. No, she had done that herself several years ago.

So why then did he feel sad? Was it because he had failed at love with her? And now, death was shoving that failure into his face, and that brought all these conflicted feelings to the surface?

He knew that she had loved him—she had told him that. Maybe he should have embraced it, given in to it, surrendered to it and let it transform him... but he just couldn't. It was too difficult. He was too set in his ways. He hadn't given in to love back then, and he wasn't going to give in to grieving about that now. He had spent too many years as a cop back in the States to let himself turn sentimental now. Years of retirement in Panama hadn't changed his nature... except, of course, for ayahuasca. He had to admit that—ayahuasca had changed him.

He checked his watch. It was time to walk down to the Taqueria and meet Ricardo. He had questions he needed to ask Ricardo. Like don Fernando, Dan needed a sounding board too.

Chapter Nine

Like most small restaurants in Panama, the seating at the Taqueria was outdoors—a couple of tables shaded by a tin roof canopy. Ricardo was already seated at one of the tables when Dan arrived.

"Did you order yet?" Dan asked him as he walked up.

"Yeah, just now," Ricardo replied. So Dan walked inside to the counter and ordered a traditional Panamanian breakfast: scrambled eggs, beans and rice, fried plantain and coffee. The cook handed him a cup of coffee, then stepped back into the kitchen to make Dan's breakfast.

Dan took his coffee over to the table where Ricardo was waiting and sat down.

"Rough night?" Ricardo asked, looking at Dan's face.

"Yeah," Dan replied.

"Bad dreams?" Ricardo asked.

"Yeah, kinda."

"Me too," Ricardo said. "I had this weird dream about Magali."

Dan felt a tiny jolt of adrenaline, but only said, "Oh? Tell me."

"It was weird," Ricardo explained, "like a dream within a dream. It started off in a train station in some foreign land. I was just standing there on the platform and I spotted her in one of the trains that was pulling out of the station. Then suddenly she was standing next to me. She dragged me over to a bench and said some stuff, and then the dream kind of ripped in two, and she was gone. Or rather, I woke up."

Dan looked at Ricardo and asked, "When you say she said some stuff, do you mean she was actually talking to you, or do you mean like in most dreams you sort of telepathically understood what she was trying to say?"

"No," Ricardo replied, "she was talking fast, like she was trying to communicate something to me."

Dan ran his finger around the rim of his coffee cup. He knew that it's not uncommon for people to dream about dead people—it happens all the time—and it certainly would not be unusual to dream of someone the night after going to their funeral. But Dan also knew that in normal dreams the dead do not speak. When the dead actually speak in dreams, it usually means that the spirit of that dead person is actually trying to connect with the living person. Spirits can speak directly to brujos, or ayahuasca users… or, Dan ruefully thought, to crazy people… but with regular people, they can only come to them through their dreaming.

"Do you remember what she said?" Dan asked.

"Yes. I got up right away and wrote it down." Ricardo pulled a piece of paper from his pocket, unfolded it and read. "She said that she was aware that she had died—she said that you told her that at the cemetery, and that she was going to visit you later on and talk with you, and that if I saw you I should tell you that I saw her."

In Dan's mind then, it was confirmed. It wasn't an ayahuasca vision he saw last night—it was Magali. Dan quietly looked at his hands as they clasped the coffee cup.

"Did she say anything else?" he asked.

"Well," Ricardo said, "she did say she didn't think she was supposed to die so early."

Dan wasn't sure what to make of that.

"Really?" he said. "Tell me the exact way she said that."

Ricardo looked at his notes again. "She just said that she didn't think she was supposed to die this early, but that she knew she was dead. Then she followed that with saying that if I saw you, I should tell you that I saw her."

"Do you know what time this dream happened?" Dan asked.

"Yes, because, like I said, we were sitting there on this bench, and then the dream kind of ripped in two, and I suddenly I was back at the funeral and then I woke up, and I got up to write it all down, so I looked at the clock. It was 11:30."

He looked at Dan, who was still staring at this coffee cup. "Did you dream about her, too?" he asked.

"Well, not exactly," Dan said. "But I didn't sleep well."

The cook brought over two plates of food to the table and placed one in front of each man.

Dan took a bite of his eggs and said, "Anyway, the reason I wanted to talk with you kind of relates to your dream... or to the part about her dying so young... What have you heard about how she died?"

"Just a lot of talk about a drug overdose," Ricardo said.

"Yeah, I heard those too," Dan said. "Did it strike you as odd? The amount of rumors about drugs?"

"Well," Ricardo said, "yeah, now that you mention it, I heard it from several people."

"Yeah, me too," said Dan. "And it struck me as odd, and at first I couldn't figure out why it seemed odd. At first I just thought it was odd because, you know, this town is so religious, especially when someone dies... It would normally be considered almost sinful to say something disrespectful about them right after they died."

"Well, the town is changing," Ricardo said.

"Yeah, maybe. But then I realized the real reason it was odd."

"Yeah? What was that?" Ricardo asked.

"It was odd because... how would they know? How would people know so fast if she had overdosed?"

Ricardo looked at Dan a little confused. "How *did* she die, Dan?"

"Well, it looked like a drug overdose, but it's a little weird.... But let me ask you one more question, and then I'll explain.... Did you ever know her to use hard drugs?"

"I never knew her to use any drugs," Ricardo said.

"Not even weed?" Dan asked

"No," Ricardo said.

"You knew she drank a lot?" Dan asked.

"Well fuck, Dan, yes—everyone in Panama drinks. But I never knew her to use anything beyond that, not even marijuana," Ricardo said.

Dan was quiet for a minute and picked at his food. Then he said, "Okay, let me tell you what's been bothering me. But this stays between me and you, okay?"

"Of course."

"So," Dan explained, "I get the call from don Fernando, saying he was at Magali's apartment and that she was dead. They hadn't even moved her body out yet—that's how soon he called me. And he said that they had found a line of white powder on the table near her body, plus a syringe with some liquid still in it, plus some other drug paraphernalia. He thought the drug stuff didn't make any sense—that Jenny would never have allowed Magali to work at her place if Magali was using drugs..."

"That's true," Ricardo interrupted. "I hadn't thought of that."

"And then," Dan continued, "he checked Magali's arms and didn't see any track marks. That's when he called me."

"Did you go over there?"

"No... I didn't want to see her like that," Dan said. "I just told him to send the syringe and the powder to the lab in Panama City, and to have one of the nurses at the ambulance service try and draw a sample of her blood and send that to the lab, too. But then later, I got to thinking about it, that it was strange that there was a line of powder and a syringe."

"What do you mean?"

"Well, I assume the line was coke, you know, laid out in a line so you could snort it.... But if you're snorting it, why have the needle? Or conversely, if you're going to inject it, why snort it?"

"Maybe it's wasn't coke," Ricardo suggested.

"Wouldn't matter," Dan said. "It wouldn't matter what it was... Most users just want to get it into their bodies in one way or another, but not both..."

"Yeah, I see what you mean."

"Yeah," Dan said, "well, hopefully we'll get the lab results back soon."

Both men ate in silence for a minute. Then Dan continued, "Anyway, later that same afternoon, I took a cab over to La Chorrera, because I wanted to talk with Jenny, to see how she was doing, and the cab driver, a fellow I don't know, asked me if I had heard about some girl overdosing in town. When I got to Jenny's, I called don Fernando and asked him to ask his men who had been at Magali's apartment if they had talked to anyone about what they had found there, and they all claimed they hadn't. So you see, it was strange that people seemed to know about it so fast. That bothered me more than anything, because you know... because things have a particular pattern—they always unfold in a particular way, like when you throw a rock in a river and the ripple always moves away from the splash in a circle... so if something unusual happens, like people knowing stuff faster than usual, it makes you wonder..."

"Yeah," said Ricardo.

"Yeah," said Dan.

Chapter Ten

Magali had never been in don Fernando's office before. In fact, she had never spoken to him. She knew who he was, of course. Everyone in Villa Rosario knew who don Fernando was, but the only contact she had ever had with him was when he had come to her mother's house that one night nine years ago to tell her mother that her husband had been killed at the sugar cane factory. Other than that, she never had any cause to interact with him because she considered herself a Christian and thus did not commit any crimes. The story around town was always that if you had to interact with don Fernando, it was never good for you.

So she wasn't sure why she wanted to see the inside of his office, but for some reason she did. It was in the back of the police station, which was located near the central park. She floated through the front desk area and down the hallway until she found it.

She was surprised at how small it was. She would have thought that someone who had been police chief of Villa Rosario for as many decades as don Fernando would have had a larger office... certainly a bigger desk and a nicer chair. But it was a tiny office, just big enough for a small desk, his chair and two chairs for visitors. On the wall was a huge map of Villa Rosario with tiny red pins stuck in various places. She floated over to the map and looked at it. Even though there were only about ten red pins in the map, as she got closer she could see thousands of tiny pin holes, where decades of pins had been stuck and removed.

She looked at the map and found the street near the outskirts of town where she had grown up. The street had no name, of course—few of the streets did. It was just a dirt road that ran alongside the Perequete River that divided Villa Rosario in half. The city limits were a few blocks north of her mother's house. Outside of the town was the neighborhood of La Pita, and further north was the city of La Chorrera.

Magali remembered taking the bus to La Chorrera a few months after her father had been killed. She remembered how she had decided to again ask Jenny for a job, so that she could help support her mother and her sisters. A few months after that, when her mother found out where she was working, she kicked Magali out of the house. Of course, that didn't stop her mother from accepting the money that Magali gave her each month out of her earnings at Jenny's. All those years of accepting money, and yet... she wouldn't even pay for Magali's funeral. When don Fernando broke the news to Magali's mother, she just told him that Jenny could damn well pay for the funeral and the mausoleum and hung up on him.

Oh well... it was of no concern to Magali now. None of that concerned her any more.

She sensed don Fernando lumbering down the hall towards his office. He was a big man and moved in a very deliberate fashion. As he walked into his office and took his seat at his desk, she was reminded of images of big rhinoceroses she had seen on TV. She looked at his face and thought that he had a rather large head—a large square head sitting on top of a thick neck. His hair was jet black and obviously dyed—it was too black to match the deep lines in his face. His mustache was dyed black as well. She imagined how he must scrutinize his mustache every morning in the mirror and decide whether to get out that little bottle of dye and that small brush and touch it up. Still... the combination of that huge head outlined by that jet back hair slicked back and that full mustache all sitting on a thick neck and a heavy body presented quite the formidable image of a man not to be trifled with. So she understood why he maintained that image. It was just part of the job. It was the same reason that she had plucked her eyebrows and shaved her public hair before going to work each night at Jenny's: to maintain an image that made the job easier. Her clients liked the young girl look. Her appearance had made it easier to extract money from her clients. Don Fernando's appearance made it easier for him to extract confessions from his clientele.

He had come into the office carrying a stack of mail. He sat down and rifled through the envelopes, looking at each return address. It appeared to Magali that he was looking for something in particular, but that it wasn't there. He frowned and then started opening each envelope, one by one, reading the contents quickly but carefully. Some of the letters went into the trash. Some he arranged in a careful pile on his desk. Magali turned around and looked at the map again, at the little curvy line that represented the street where she had lived as a child. She did not want to visit that house again... no one really does... no one wants to see how they grew up... we only keep certain images in our minds—sweet memories... not the poverty, the desolation, the loneliness, the feeling that every child has at one point or another looking around and realizing that nothing but more poverty and loneliness lay ahead... no one wants to re-experience that... and yet, everyone has this feeling of wanting—of longing—to return to a home, a home that never really existed... And so it was with Magali. She floated out of don Fernando's office and out past the front lobby.

Once outside of the police station, she let herself rise up and float over the large central park bordered by the police station at one end and the towering Catholic Church at the other. Like all Panamanian towns, Villa Rosario was laid out around a huge central park—a park that took up a complete city block. Cement walkways crisscrossed the park. Concrete benches sat in the shade under huge mango and palm trees. Green parrots sang in the trees. At the center of the park was a large fountain where pigeons and children played. Mothers and grandmothers sat on the concrete benches and gossiped while the children chased the pigeons or each other. A few souvenir vendors tried selling trinkets to the gringos walking through the park. Official and pirate taxi drivers lined up at their respective corners of the park, waiting for customers.

Magali followed the Perequete River north to her old neighborhood. The streets looked exactly the same as when she had grown up—dirt streets with large ruts. There was no breeze, and the humid air hung in the street like the smell of dirty clothes. Stray dogs lounged wherever they could find shade. Dog shit was everywhere. Even the houses looked exactly the same—as if they would collapse at any moment. Rusty tin roofs, occasional old broken tile roofs, sometimes just plastic sheets held in place with rocks... Villa Rosario was a poor town, but this was the poor section of town. Up the road, Magali could see the shack where she had grown up. She looked at how tiny it was, now much it resembled a piece of trash left by the roadside... the trees were taller now... there were different cars parked in front... but it was the same hovel. Some shirts and a pair of blue jeans were drying on a line that was strung from the front door to a barbed-wire fence. The front window where she used to look out of was broken. There were chickens in the front yard... chickens... chickens...

An old memory floated by. Magali looked at it. She was seven years old. Her father was beating her with a paddle because she wouldn't help him kill some of the chickens. They had been her pets—or so she thought at the time—but she had walked into the back yard and her father was holding one by the throat and jabbing a long knife into its mouth and into its brain to kill it for dinner. Magali had screamed and started to cry. Her father dropped the dead chicken and grabbed Magali's arm and told her it was time to grow up and learn how to kill chickens. Magali screamed louder and so her father started beating her...

Magali didn't need to see any more. She could leave this all behind now. She turned around and let herself drift back to the center of town.

Thank God she was dead.

Chapter Eleven

It was three days later that don Fernando finally received the large manila envelope he had been waiting for. He opened it as he stepped from the front lobby to go back to his office. He scanned the first two paragraphs as he was walking, but when he got to the third paragraph he suddenly stopped and just stood there in the middle of the hallway and read the rest of the report. Then he folded it, slid it back in the envelope and just stood there, thinking. A couple of his officers at the other end of the hallway saw him standing there and gave each other a questioning look. One of them was about to take a step down the hallway to ask don Fernando if everything was okay, but the other officer stopped him and just shook his head no. Both officers returned to their duties in the front lobby. After another minute, don Fernando went into his office and called Dan.

As soon as Dan picked up the phone, don Fernando started talking.

"Dani, this is Fernando. Can you come down to the station and see me?"

"What?"

"Can you come down to the station?"

"Now?" Dan asked.

"Yes, Dani. I need to talk with you."

"I'm still in bed, don Fernando!"

"Please, mi amigo, this is important."

"Ah, fuck..." Dan said. "Okay, give me a few minutes..."

Dan pulled himself out of bed and threw yesterday's clothes on. He splashed water on his face but didn't bother shaving. In fact, he hadn't shaved in a few days. Since

Magali's visit four nights earlier, Dan had stopped drinking ayahuasca, but had substituted whiskey instead. He hadn't been on a complete bender, but clearly he was trying to blot out something. He knew the ayahuasca made it easier for Magali to return, and something about that scared him. The whiskey somehow seemed to make him more ghost-proof.

He walked downtown, through the central park and into the police station. The sergeant at the front desk looked up when Dan walked in. Although he recognized Dan, the sergeant's frown let Dan know he probably looked like shit. Dan just pointed down the hall towards don Fernando's office, and the desk sergeant nodded and went back to his work.

"Okay, I'm here," Dan said as he stepped into don Fernando's office.

Don Fernando looked at his friend, but said nothing about his appearance.

"Dani, I received the lab report on that girl today."

Dan stiffened up. "On Magali?" he asked.

"Yes. She died of an overdose of burundanga," don Fernando said.

Dan was confused. He had heard the word before, but couldn't remember where.

"I don't know what that is, don Fernando."

"A drug from Colombia, Dani."

Dan still felt in the dark, so he asked, "What else was in her system?"

"Nothing. Just burundanga—a dose large enough to kill."

"Was that what the powder on the table was?" Dan asked

Don Fernando shook his head no.

"No, that was cocaine.... And the syringe was heroin."

"I don't understand, don Fernando."

"She was murdered, Dani," don Fernando said. "And someone tried to make it look like an accidental overdose."

Don Fernando slid the lab report across the desk.

Dan picked it up and started to read it. It was in Spanish, of course, but Dan's Spanish was good enough to get through it. He got to the paragraph that identified the drug found in Magali's blood.

"La escopolamina?" Dan said out loud.

"That's the medical name for burundanga," don Fernando said.

Then it clicked for Dan. Escopolamina, the Spanish word for scopolamine... burundanga... the Devil's Breath flower... a pretty white trumpet-like flower that grew wild in Colombia. Dan had heard about it years ago from old brujos. Burundanga was a drug that was known for centuries to the indigenous medicine men, but it was not commonly used. In small doses, it induced a zombie-like trance. In large doses, it brought death. Brujos had no use for it—they preferred ayahuasca or peyote. Burundanga was unpredictable and had no religious or oracular powers. But it was used by the *malignos*—those fake brujos who practiced black magic— and more recently by criminals in Colombia. They would make a powder from the seeds of the flower and then blow it into a tourist's face or pour it anywhere on their skin. That was the thing that made burundanga so dangerous—it was absorbed through the skin almost immediately. Depending on the amount used, the victim would be incoherent or passed out in a matter of seconds and could be easily robbed. Burundanga also induced a type of amnesia. When the victim woke—if they woke—they would have no memory of what happened.

"What's scopolamine doing in Panama?" Dan asked.

"Ah Dani, that is what worries me," don Fernando said. "Devil's Breath does not grow this far north. So someone would have had to bring the powder here from Colombia, and the only people who make that powder are criminal gangs."

"Well, maybe it wasn't burundanga, don Fernando. Maybe it was prescription scopolamine," Dan suggested.

"No Dani, I called Dr. Vargas who wrote the report.

She said it was not a synthetic drug in the girl's blood. She said it was organic, with a lot of impurities. She wrote 'la escopolomina' in the report, but she told me she thought it was burundanga from Colombia."

Dan turned to the last page of the report. Yes, Dr. Vargas had signed it. Dan remembered her—María José Vargas—the head toxicologist at the Ministry of Justice's Forensic Laboratory in Panama City. She had helped him and don Fernando on a case a few years back. Dan had remembered her not only for being attractive but for also being a very thorough scientist. If she said it was burundanga, then that's what it was.

Dan turned back to the first page of the report and read through it. Don Fernando was correct—the only drug in Magali's body was a lethal amount of scopolamine. No other drugs. No wonder don Fernando concluded she had been murdered. Someone poured out a line of coke on her table and left a syringe half-full of heroin on her table to make it look like suicide or an accidental overdose. That's why there were no track marks on her arms, and that's why Jenny had never noticed any odd behavior—because Magali didn't use drugs.

Dan put the report down and closed his eyes. He willed himself to not feel anything emotional, and to only use what was left of his cop brain to think about this. He needed his cop brain—because it made no sense that someone would murder Magali.

"Don Fernando," Dan asked. "Was her apartment dusted for fingerprints?"

Don Fernando just shook his head no.

"Was there any evidence of a robbery?"

"No, Dani. There was money in her purse, and nothing appeared to have been taken."

Dan tried to think of all the possibilities. Could the drug have been hers and she accidently ingested it? No, because then there would not have been the other drugs on the table. A burglary gone wrong? Possibly. But again, why leave the syringe? Someone seeking revenge? It was hard to think that Magali would have any enemies. Maybe a crazy client?

"Did Magali see customers at her house?" Dan asked.

"I do not know, Dani. I am going to go to La Chorrera this afternoon and interview Jenny."

"Has anyone been to her apartment since she died?"

"I don't believe so," don Fernando said.

"Then let's go now," Dan said. "Let's go take a look. Do you have someone who can dust for fingerprints?"

"I think Vicente is working today," don Fernando said, and picked up the phone.

*　*　*

But when don Fernando, Dan, and Vicente arrived at Magali's apartment and opened the door, the apartment was empty. The table, bed, chairs... everything was gone. The three men walked through the apartment. It was completely empty.

"The landlord lives in the house next door," don Fernando said to Dan. "Let's go there. Vicente, you stay here and dust the light switches and door jams."

"Sí, Capitán," Vicente responded.

Dan and don Fernando walked around the block to a small house and rang the doorbell. An older man peered through the window, looking annoyed, but then saw it was don Fernando. Then, he quickly came outside.

"Sí, don Fernando," the old man asked, "how can I help you?"

"What happened to the apartment of the dead girl?" don Fernando asked brusquely.

"Her family came by yesterday and took everything out," the old man said. "They said that they were her only heirs, so it all belonged to them."

Don Fernando frowned.

"I am sorry, don Fernando, I thought you were done

56

with the apartment," the old man said apologetically.

Don Fernando just nodded.

"Did they leave any trash behind?" Dan asked. "Any garbage bags?"

"Sí, a few, but the garbage men came by this morning and took all the trash away."

"Who exactly was here yesterday?" don Fernando asked.

"Well, there was her mother—I recognized her... and a man she called Hernán... I think he is a boyfriend... and some other man I didn't know, who was helping them."

"Did they ever come here before?" don Fernando asked.

"I do not know, don Fernando," the old man replied. "I know the mother from town—that's all. I never saw them here before."

"What about other visitors?" Dan asked. "Did people come to visit her?"

The old man lowered his head and said, "I do not pry into my tenants' affairs, señor. I never saw anyone. She paid her rent on time, was always quiet... never a problem..."

Don Fernando looked at the old man, then said, "You knew she worked at Jenny's in La Chorrera." It was a statement, not a question. The old man just nodded yes.

Don Fernando scratched his chin, then asked, "This man, Hernán... local?"

"I had never seen him before."

"Was he a panameño?" don Fernando asked.

"That was not my impression, don Fernando. But I did not hear him speak, so I cannot say."

"What did he look like?" don Fernando asked.

"He was skinny, tall, dark... *indio*," the old man said, using the Spanish for Indian.

"Hmmm... and what made you think he was the boyfriend of the girl's mother?" don Fernando asked.

"Just the way she deferred to him," the old man said.

"Okay. Thank you, señor. If any of them come back,

would you let me know?"

"Of course, don Fernando, of course."

As they walked back to Magali's apartment, don Fernando said to Dan, "You know, Dani, the name Hernán is not a common name in Panama..."

"Yeah?" Dan said.

"But it is common in Colombia..."

Dan looked at don Fernando but didn't say anything. He was thinking. Dan never liked to jump to conclusions about a case. Maybe it was just a coincidence that Magali's mother and her friends showed up so fast to claim all the furniture. After all, they were poor and could make some quick cash by selling those things. And maybe it was just a speculation that this boyfriend was Colombian—the same country that burundanga comes from. It was true that Hernán was not a common Panamanian name, but it was not unheard of... Dan filed all these things away, like pieces to a puzzle. There were still too many pieces missing.

Vicente came outside Magali's apartment as the two men walked up. He looked at don Fernando and just shook his head.

"There are no prints anywhere, Capitán. Everything has been wiped clean."

"Nothing at all?" don Fernando asked.

"No, Capitán. I dusted every light switch, every door, even the knobs on the stove. Everything was scrubbed clean."

Don Fernando turned and looked at Dan, arched one eyebrow, but said nothing.

Chapter Twelve

That afternoon, don Fernando drove up to La Chorrera to see Jenny. The brothel didn't open until evening, so they could have met there. Jenny had known don Fernando for decades and had no secrets from him, but she always preferred that police cars never be seen parked near her establishment—she thought it might scare away customers—so she suggested they meet at the Café Sueño downtown. They found a quiet corner table where they could talk. The waiter knew Jenny and automatically brought her hot tea. Don Fernando ordered a coffee with sugar.

As was customary in Panama, they chatted for the first fifteen minutes about their families, their spouses, their health, and recent events. Gradually, the conversation came around to Magali and the recent funeral.

"Actually, *mi reina*, that is one of the reasons I wanted to visit you," don Fernando said. "The death of this girl nags at me. She was too young, and that troubles me. Tell me: had she been acting strange lately, had any problems lately?"

"No, don Fernando, she seemed herself. Magali was not… well, she wasn't someone who revealed her feelings much. But this death came as a shock to me. I thought I knew her as well as anyone could… I guess I didn't know her at all… If I had known she was having some kind of problem, maybe I could have helped, but she seemed normal."

"Any problems with clients? Or fights with any friends?" don Fernando asked.

Jenny just shook her head no.

"Did she have a boyfriend?"

"No. She was close to Antonia. That was why I asked Antonia to go check on her that morning—because they were close. If I had known what Antonia was going to find, I never would have sent her. She's in such pain."

"I wanted to chat with this Antonia. Is she working tonight?" don Fernando asked.

"No. She hasn't been able to work since that morning. She just stays in her apartment and cries. I took her some soup for lunch today."

"What about clients? Did Magali have any new clients recently?"

Jenny looked at don Fernando and asked, "Oh, you have suspicions about Magali's death?"

"I do."

"Don Fernando, I thought I was going crazy," Jenny blurted, "because I do, too! It just made no sense. When I heard she overdosed, I couldn't believe it."

"What exactly did you hear, Jenny?" don Fernando asked.

"That the police found needles... but I didn't believe that. I would have known if she was using drugs, don Fernando. You know my business. I have a nurse check all the girls once a month. If Magali had been using drugs, especially needles, either I or the nurse would have spotted it."

"Who told you these stories?" don Fernando asked.

Jenny tried to think where she had heard them. She shrugged and said, "In my line of work, don Fernando, a lot of people gossip with me... Sometimes it's useful information, sometimes not. But I always listen—I need to know who's around, who's trustworthy, who's trouble... I think I heard this story first from a girl named Luna. She's an independent, works the hotel bars. She told me she heard it from a pimp named Rodriguez. His brother owns a bar called Ébano on Calle del Puerto, and Rodriguez runs a few girls in the back of the bar in the evenings. Luna is okay—not that bright, but okay—but Rodriguez is scum, so I didn't believe it. But then the other night I heard it from a customer."

"Who was that?" don Fernando asked.

"A fellow from Villa Rosario named Lucas."

"What can you tell me about him?"

"He works in a truck repair shop on the east side of Villa Rosario."

Don Fernando thought for a minute. "Is he short, fat, bald?"

"Yes."

"Lucas Antigua Martin?" don Fernando asked.

"That's him."

"And what did he say?"

"Just that he had heard that Magali had overdosed on drugs and that he was sorry—that he had always liked her," Jenny said.

"Did he say anything about needles?" don Fernando asked.

"Well, no... but what he said was that he had heard that she had overdosed by shooting up drugs... that's what made me think he was talking about needles."

Jenny paused for a minute and then asked, "Did she overdose by needle, don Fernando?"

"No."

"How did she die?"

Don Fernando took a breath and said, "I will this in strict confidence Jenny... All I really know right now is that there *were* drugs in her system, and that's how she died. Beyond that... we're still investigating. So keep this to yourself."

"Of course, don Fernando, of course."

"Was Lucas Antigua Martin a customer of Magali's?" don Fernando asked.

"Occasionally, but he did not have any preferences. He would take whoever was available."

"Yes," Don Fernando thought to himself, "that figures." Lucas was not an attractive man, and was very shy.

"What about any other customers—anyone new lately? Anyone causing any problems?"

"Just the usual regulars, and a steady parade of

gringos passing through, but no problems recently."

"And this Antonia girl," don Fernando said. "Tell me about her."

"She's nice girl, from the country. Not much education, but not stupid. She has worked for me for about six months, maybe seven. She and Magali got along well. Antonia prefers women."

"Any criminal history? Bad habits?" don Fernando asked.

"No, she's a good girl."

Don Fernando finished his coffee. He had no more questions to ask Jenny. But he was interested in this Rodriguez fellow. As long as he was in La Chorrera, don Fernando thought he might pay him a visit.

"I think that's all the questions I have, Jenny," he said. But then, almost on a whim, he asked, "By the way, have any colombianos or indios foreigners come by the brothel recently?"

"Well... yes," Jenny said, "there was one, about a week or so ago, a skinny dark man came by, but I did not let him stay. I interviewed him and had a bad feeling about him after just a few sentences—he seemed a little crazy. So I told him I didn't have anyone for him and that he had to leave. You know me... if I don't like someone, I won't introduce them to my girls. My intuition about men is usually right."

"And what did your intuition tell you about this fellow?" don Fernando asked.

"That he was a loose cannon. Most men are nervous the first time at a place, you know. But this guy was just too controlled, and I could feel that there was something bad underneath."

Jenny shrugged, then added, "What can I say? I just didn't like him."

"Do you remember his name?"

Jenny squinted her eyes and looked left and then down. "Hyram... no, Hernán. His name was Hernán."

"Did you get his full name?"

"No," Jenny said, "he was only here a minute or two. I talked to him at the doorway. I didn't even let him come into the living room—that's how fast I didn't like him."

"Not a local?"

"Oh definitely not. I had never seen him before. At the time I thought his accent was Colombian... I don't remember why... oh, yes I do. He told me his friend had told him about my place, but he used the word 'cuadro' for friend—and we certainly don't use that slang here, but they do in Colombia."

Don Fernando nodded his head. He had heard that slang before.

Chapter Thirteen

Don Fernando wanted to find out what this Rodriguez fellow knew. If this had been Villa Rosario, he simply would have hauled the guy in and squeezed the information out of him. But this was La Chorrera, and don Fernando didn't have jurisdiction here. He had to first go through his nephew, Jorge Manuel, who was the police chief of La Chorrera.

So don Fernando drove over to the La Chorrera police station and called Jorge Manuel on the way.

"Koke," he said, addressing Jorge Manuel by his family nickname. "It's Fernando. I'm in your town this afternoon, and I need a favor from you."

"Of course, uncle, a su servicio," Jorge Manuel replied.

"There's a witness I want to interview, a man who works at a bar called Ébano over on Calle del Puerto."

"Hmmm, a rough place, uncle," Jorge Manuel said.

"That's okay," said don Fernando. "Can you spare me thirty minutes?"

"Of course."

"Good. I'll park at your office in a few minutes. Let's take one of your squad cars."

* * *

On the drive over to the Ébano Bar, don Fernando gave his nephew a shorthand version of the situation.

"So, Koke, we find this dead girl five days ago, and within hours it's all over town that we had found drugs and a syringe at her apartment. But my men swear they didn't tell anyone about what we had found. I think the drugs were planted to make it look like an overdose, and someone is spreading rumors that this girl was a drug user...”

“How did she die, uncle?” Jorge Manuel asked.

“Well... it *was* drugs, but it was different... I’ll explain about that later... but the point is, I think someone is spreading rumors, because even here in La Chorrera, people are talking about it. I had coffee with Jenny this afternoon, and she heard the rumor from some streetwalker who heard it from this pimp named Rodriguez. Rodriguez’s brother owns the Ébano Bar, and evidently Rodriguez runs a few whores in the back. Now, I just want to put a little heat on this guy... I don’t want to mention the dead girl at all... in fact, I want him to assume that we think she *did* use drugs and that there’s a new source of heroin and cocaine in town, and that somehow we think he’s involved... maybe if he gets nervous, we may learn something.”

“Okay,” said Jorge Manuel. “What do you want me to do when we get there?”

“Nothing,” said don Fernando. “Just say nothing and look tough. I just want to scare the guy.”

“Okay.”

Don Fernando directed Jorge Manuel to park the police car directly in front of the Ébano Bar, and they walked inside. His nephew was right, don Fernando thought, this was a rough place. The bar was full of hard drinkers. The place was dark, and it stank. But don Fernando also knew the power of image: Jorge Manuel had his police uniform on and was armed. Don Fernando was wearing his usual dark suit and tie, but his massive frame still presented a formidable presence. The men at the bar looked around but didn’t make any eye contact. Don Fernando assumed some of them had warrants out.

Don Fernando walked up to the bar. The bartender came right over.

“Sí, señor?”

“The owner,” was all don Fernando said.

“Sí, señor,” the bartender said, and quickly walked

toward the back. He returned a few seconds later with a short stocky man who had a concerned look on his face.

"Sí, señor?"

"Your brother Rodriguez is here?" don Fernando said.

The man looked around, a bit more concerned. "He's in the back. I'll get him."

"No," don Fernando said, "take us to him."

"Well, he's busy," the man protested.

"Take us to him ... now," don Fernando said slowly.

Jorge Manuel moved his hand to his gun.

"This way," the man said.

As the three men walked to the back of the bar, don Fernando heard one of the men at the bar laugh and say, "Rodriguez is in trouble." Everyone always relaxes when it's someone else's trouble, don Fernando thought.

In the back of the bar was a hallway lined with doors. It was a standard whore bar set-up. Behind each door would be a room no bigger than a closet—just big enough for a metal bed frame and a thin mattress. Just enough room for a quick fuck or blowjob. The hallway was empty, but the evening was young. Don Fernando guessed that there would only be one or two older whores working this shift. The younger women—and "younger" would only be a relative term in a dive like this—would arrive later in the evening.

At the end of the hallway, the bar owner knocked on the last door.

"What?" came a male voice from inside the room.

"Some gentlemen here to see you, Rodriguez," the owner said.

"Tell them to wait at the bar with the others—I'm busy right now," came an irritated reply.

"These are policía," said the owner.

There was a shuffling from behind the closed door, and a short man with a scruffy beard poked his head out of the door. When he saw the uniformed Jorge Manuel and don Fernando standing there, his eyes widened. "Just a minute," he mumbled, and pulled his head back into the room. Then he stepped out from behind the door, adjusting his clothes and carefully closing the door behind him so no one could see inside.

"Sí, señores, what can I do for you?"

Don Fernando looked at the bar owner and said, "You can go now." The man scurried away. When he was out of sight, don Fernando looked at the man in front of him.

"You are Rodriguez?"

"Sí."

Don Fernando reached out slowly with his large left hand, gently grabbed Rodriguez by the throat and eased him back against the door. With his right hand, he patted around Rodriguez's waistband to make sure he had no gun. Even so, he kept his left hand on Rodriguez's throat and lifted Rodriguez's head slightly upwards.

"Señor Rodriguez, we have information that you are involved with bringing in a new line of product into the town of Villa Rosario..."

Don Rodriguez tightened his grip on Rodriguez throat slightly and lifted him slightly higher.

"That product," don Fernando continued, "being heroin and cocaine. Now, I run a nice quiet town over in Villa Rosario, and the way I deal with drug dealers is that I simply kill them..."

Jorge Manuel, for his part, had gotten used to don Fernando's methods years ago. He knew that don Fernando did not, in fact, kill drug dealers—unless of course it was absolutely necessary—but that he used his reputation to scare drug dealers away from Villa Rosario. So none of this discussion surprised or concerned Jorge Manuel. He just kept his stare directly on this scruffy young man, playing the part of La Chorrera's counterpart to don Fernando.

"Señor, señor," Rodriguez sputtered, "you are mistaken. I do not deal in any type of drugs."

"That's not what we hear, Rodriguez," don Fernando said. "We hear you're helping malignos move heroin and cocaine into my quiet little town."

"No, no, I don't know what you're talking about, I swear!" Rodriguez exclaimed. "I am no narcotraficante!"

Don Fernando forced Rodriguez's head higher, so Rodriguez was up on his tiptoes.

"Don't lie to me you little pimp!" don Fernando spit out. "We have witnesses who have watched you working with these men in Villa Rosario!"

"No, no, I was just visiting a friend of mine from Colombia."

"Oh yeah?" Don Fernando was yelling now. "And your friend Hernán gave you a little taste of what he's bringing in, didn't he?"

"No señor, I swear it! He gave me nothing. We just talked, that's all."

Don Fernando relaxed his grip on Rodriguez's throat. "Listen to me, you little piece of shit, we've got spies all over Villa Rosario. If I see you in my town again, you won't leave alive. And if we hear of you dealing any drugs here in La Chorrera, you'll wish you were dead."

Don Fernando let go of Rodriguez's neck. Rodriguez backed up, rubbing his neck, coughing and breathing hard. Don Fernando pushed him aside and opened the door that Rodriguez had so carefully closed. A fat naked middle-aged woman was sitting scrunched up on the bed, her arms wrapped around her thick legs, her eyes staring wide in fear at don Fernando. Don Fernando closed the door, shook his head in disapproval, and said to Jorge Manuel, "Come on, let's get out of this shit hole." And the two police officers walked down the hallway, out past the bar, and out to Jorge Manuel's patrol car.

As Jorge Manuel drove them back to the police station, don Fernando was deep in thought. Maybe he shouldn't have roughed-up that punk. He had learned some things—he had confirmed that Hernán was Colombian and that Rodriguez had visited him in Villa Rosario. But in questioning Rodriguez, he had now alerted Hernán that the police were interested in him—for no doubt Rodriguez would be phoning Hernán telling him about this visit. This would have been enough in the old days. This would have sent a message—a warning—to wannabe drug dealers to clear out of town. But the old days were gone. And these weren't punks from Panama City coming to Villa Rosario to sell marijuana. These were Colombians with burundanga and heroin and cocaine, the drugs of cartels... and cartels had *sicarios*—hitmen who had no hesitation in assassinating young girls or old policemen. No, maybe he was wrong to have played his hand so early... but what other choice did he have?   If he hadn't have talked to Rodriguez, he wouldn't have been able to connect the dots between the rumors about the dead girl, the appearance of this Hernán fellow from Colombia, and the fact that the girl was killed with burundanga.... "connect the dots"... that was Dani's favorite expression... yes, he needed to talk to Dani soon.

Jorge Manuel could sense that his uncle was worried as they rode in silence back to the police station.

"Would you like to stay for dinner, uncle?" Jorge Manuel asked. "Marina and the kids would love to see you."

"No, gracias, Koke. Some other day perhaps," don Fernando replied. "But I do need to explain this case more to you, so if you have a few more minutes... when we get to your office..."

"Of course, uncle."

Chapter Fourteen

Back in Jorge Manuel's office, don Fernando explained to his nephew how Magali had been poisoned by burundanga, and not by the heroin and cocaine found on the table in her apartment. He told him how Magali's mother had come with two men and cleaned out Magali's apartment, and that one of the men was named Hernán—the same name as the man who Jenny was suspicious about—and the same name that Rodriguez seemed to say was his Colombian friend in Villa Rosario. Jorge Manuel listened without saying a word. He had been appointed police chief of La Chorrera several years ago, because of don Fernando's influence on the city fathers, but the fact was he was inexperienced in dealing with sophisticated crimes. Over the years he always had to enlist don Fernando's help when he felt like he was in over his head... and occasionally don Fernando had brought his friend Dan Landes along. Jorge Manuel was grateful for both men's help.

"So, Koke," don Fernando was saying. "I think there are colombianos moving into our country, but I don't know if they are part of an organized narcotráfico cartel, or just some renegade malignos. Their methods make no sense to me. At first, I thought they might be using the Devil's Breath to eliminate competition. But this girl was no competition... and it made no sense to stage her apartment as if she was a drug user..."

"Maybe they were trying to send a message to someone else?" Jorge Manuel suggested.

"Maybe, Koke, maybe... but to whom? Dani is equally baffled. He even said that they may just be very stupid criminals—that it was strange to leave both cocaine and heroin on the table."

"So, you've talked to Señor Landes?" Jorge Manuel asked.

"Sí, I called him as soon as we found the dead girl," don Fernando replied.

"And he has no ideas, no suggestions?"

"Well, Koke, I could tell he was very upset. He used to be close to his girl... maybe closer than I realized. I felt badly when I saw him at the funeral... but to answer your question, he suggested we start doing blood analysis on every death that looks like an overdose or even natural causes. I called María José Vargas at the forensic laboratory in Panama City and told her to expect more specimens from both of our cities. She said she would start testing crime scene blood from other cities for burundanga as well."

Jorge Manuel just nodded his head.

"Dani also asked me if we had seen more heroin or cocaine arrests recently. I told him that over the past few years it has been steadily getting worse, but that we hadn't seen any sudden increase recently. Have you?"

"No uncle, no more than usual. Most of our arrests have been couriers moving product through Panama to the north. It's a steady business, but you know how it is—they want to sell the drugs to gringos in the United States. Our people can't afford them. The only reason drugs even get distributed here is because the cartels pay the couriers in drugs rather than money."

Don Fernando nodded and said, "That's what I told Dani. Anyway, he asked that we both keep track of how much drugs we catch coming through this area, both the amounts and the locations, and to let him know each week."

"I'll send you a weekly report, uncle."

"Thank you, Koke... You know, this used to be such a nice country... but lately, I don't know."

"It's the price of progress, uncle," Jorge Manuel shrugged. "We have many more condos now and many more gringos. The local merchants are making more money, but there is more crime, more problems…"

Don Fernando frowned and thought for a minute. Then he said, almost thinking out loud, "You must have many more gringos here than we do in Villa Rosario…"

Jorge nodded and said, "Since they started building those condos on the east side, we have been flooded with gringos… too many, really…"

"I wonder if they use drugs," don Fernando said softly, rubbing his chin.

"Most of them are retired, uncle… you know, older gringos."

"Well, maybe if you have a chance, Koke, you could just visit those condos and see if they all look old or if they are some younger gringos living there, too."

"Okay, uncle."

"Well Koke, I'm going to head back home," don Fernando said as he stood up. "I thank you for your hospitality today. We'll talk soon."

"No problem, uncle, anytime."

Don Fernando walked out of the La Chorrera police station and muttered to himself again, "This used to be such a nice country."

Chapter Fifteen

The next day, don Fernando drove over to the northeast section of town to visit Magali's mother. He knew that interviewing her would be require a far more subtle touch than his little chat with Rodriguez. Don Fernando did not believe for a second that she felt any loss for Magali other than the loss of whatever money Magali gave her. However, as a "bereaved mother", a *viuda,* and a *doña* resident of Villa Rosario, she was entitled to a certain respect. However, it would not be inappropriate for the police chief to drop by her house on a condolence call a few days after the funeral, which was exactly how don Fernando planned to play it.

The particular neighborhood where Magali's mother lived didn't have an official name, but the residents referred to it as *la Pitalita* since it was so near the neighborhood of *La Pita*, which lay just outside of the city boundaries of Villa Rosario. The police didn't get many calls to come to this neighborhood—this was one of those poor but tight-knit barrios that took care of its own problems... If some thief got caught breaking into a house here, the neighbors would get together and the robber would simply disappear, and his body would never be found.

Don Fernando drove slowly up the pot-holed dirt road. It had been nine years since he had last driven this road, and that journey had also been a condolence visit—to tell Magali's mother that her husband had been killed in an accident at the sugar cane mill.

As a courtesy—and more so as a practicality—don Fernando had taken an unmarked police car from the station. He parked in front of a shack with a green front, tin siding and a tin roof, with a small broken fence lining the yard. A woman who was hanging wash out to dry in front of the house turned and looked to see who had driven up. Even though it had been nine years, don Fernando recognized her.

"Hola, doña Rosa," he said, addressing Magali's mother with the term of respect. "¿Cómo está?"

Rosa seemed taken back. It had been nine years, but everyone in Villa Rosario knew who don Fernando was. His was not a face you forgot. But she recovered quickly. "I am well, don Fernando, I mean… under the circumstances."

"I understand, doña Rosa. I simply came to pay my condolences for your loss. I knew you were inconsolable, too upset to attend the funeral. So I decided to wait a few days before paying my respects.

Rosa appeared to relax a bit. "That was kind of you, don Fernando," she said.

"Well, I know it was a terrible loss," don Fernando added.

"Yes… yes, it was… a terrible loss… but you know, don Fernando, these young people, they bring their problems on themselves when they start messing with the drugs," Rosa said.

"Yes, that's true," don Fernando said, in a sympathetic tone. "Once they get hooked on drugs, it's all downhill. It's a terrible problem."

"Yes," Rosa said.

"They start off just experimenting, but then they start using more and more," don Fernando said "And even though everyone knows they're using and tells them to stop, they keep right on using."

"Yes, exactly!" Rosa said.

"Was Magali using drugs for a long time?" don Fernando asked.

"I think so, don Fernando, ever since she started working for *that woman*." Rosa spit out the last two words like a curse.

"Ah yes, over in La Chorrera," don Fernando said

in a tone that implied that those issues were outside his jurisdiction.

"Yes, that one," Rosa said.

"What about here in la Pitalita, doña Rosa? Are there more drugs circulating here?"

"No don Fernando, not here. This is a poor neighborhood, but *gracias a Dios* we don't have a drug problem here. No one can afford drugs here."

"So, you think Magali was getting her drugs somewhere else in Villa Rosario?"

"No, I think she was getting them all from La Chorrera," Rosa answered. "Every time I saw her, she was high."

Don Fernando knew Rosa was lying, because he knew what Dan and Ricardo knew—that Jenny would have fired Magali in a heartbeat if she had been using drugs. But he continued to nod his head sympathetically and said, "A terrible thing, doña Rosa, a terrible thing... When was the last time you saw Magali?"

"Oh... um, recently, don Fernando, recently... I don't remember the exact date, but we were close; we visited regularly."

Another lie, don Fernando thought. Everyone knew that Magali and her mother were estranged.

"By the way, doña Rosa, the apartment manager told me that you and your friends came by her apartment a few days ago to collect her things."

Don Fernando sensed that she stiffened imperceptibly when he said that, so he quickly added, "I was glad to see you were able to get all that furniture out. No sense in letting it go to waste. If you hadn't taken it, the landlord would probably just have sold it."

"Yes, yes, well that's what we thought," Rosa said. "We are poor here, as you know, don Fernando, and any money helps."

"It's a good thing you had friends to help you move those bigger pieces. They looked quite heavy."

"Yes, they were."

"Did Lucas Antigua Martin help you?"

"Yes, don Fernando, how did you know?"

"Well, I just figured... you know, him being nearby, and having all those trucks. You would have needed a truck to move all that furniture."

"Yes, yes, well it was nice of him to offer to help," Rosa said.

"And the other man who helped you, who was he?"

"Oh... some friend of Lucas... I don't remember his name."

"Ah... a newcomer to town?"

"Yes, yes, I think so."

"And where does he live, doña Rosa?"

"Oh... I don't know, don Fernando, I only saw him that one day."

Again, don Fernando had the distinct feeling she was lying to him. She started fidgeting with the clothes pins in her hands.

"Well, no matter," don Fernando said. "It was good you had help. I wish more people would help each other out in this world."

"Yes, don Fernando, I agree."

Don Fernando looked at the wet clothes that Rosa had hung on the line. He noticed a man's shirt and underwear.

"The rest of your children, doña Rosa, they are well?" he asked.

"Yes, *gracias a Dios*, they are well."

"Ah, that is good. They have all moved out, right? None of them live at home now?"

"No, don Fernando, they have all grown and moved out."

"Ah, you have the whole house to yourself then, doña Rosa. Do your children visit often?"

"Well, no, don Fernando, I don't see them often. They all have their own lives, you know."

"Yes, yes, I understand, well, it must get lonesome

then, being here all by yourself. Are you able perhaps to rent one of the rooms out?"

"No, no, I prefer to live alone," Rosa said.

"Yes, I understand, doña Rosa, I understand... Well, I must be going. I just wanted to stop by and pay my respects."

"Yes, thank you again, don Fernando. You are very kind."

Don Fernando smiled, and got back into his car. As he drove away, he watched Rosa in the rear-view mirror as she pulled a cell phone out of her pocket and began to dial. He thought back over the conversation and concluded that every word out of her mouth had been a lie.

Chapter Sixteen

Slowly, Magali began to understand that she must be searching for something... but she didn't know what it was. At first she thought that she was merely curious, and that was why she floated from neighborhood to neighborhood, floating through the houses, looking at all the people. But then she realized that she was being pulled along, as if by a current, pulling her gently in its slipstream, taking her through the neighborhoods, through the houses... as if searching for something or someone. But what it was she was searching for, Magali just didn't know. Nor did she care. She found the places and the people interesting—so many faces, so many stories, so many tragedies. It was almost incomprehensible how many different stories people lived, how many different fates were all unfolding at the same time...

On most nights, she would return to Antonia's little apartment and would watch her sleep. Sometimes, she would let herself float down through the thin blanket and curl up like smoke around Antonia's body. Sometimes she would enter Antonia's dreams, just to watch her move.

But the more nights that Magali spent with Antonia, the more she was filled with that most bittersweet sorrow— the kind of sorrow that can only come from realizing too late how much you had loved someone, realizing too late that you had held back and not given in to love, had not let yourself fall completely and irretrievably in love... and that now it was too late.

But it wasn't Antonia she was searching for. Magali accepted that the opportunity to love was forever gone. Her nightly visits only served to drink in the memory once more, but she knew that human love was no longer possible. The nights simply provided relief from whatever currents were carrying her through the day... because it was in the daytime that she was aware of searching, or rather, that she was aware of being pulled around Villa Rosario as if she was searching for something.

The currents seemed to always circle around her old neighborhood near the Perequete River. She did not want to see her old house again, and the currents seemed to understand that, and pulled her around all the streets near her neighborhood, without ever taking her back to the house where she grew up. Those surrounding streets held happier memories, for they were the streets she walked through as a child on her way to school, or to see playmates, or to just walk anywhere that took her away from the house of sorrows that was her home.

And each night she returned to Antonia's apartment and let herself envelop Antonia's sleeping body. It occurred to Magali that Antonia must not be working at Jenny's because she was always home.

Magali was glad of that.

She began entering Antonia's dreams more and more. At first, she only watched Antonia's dreams, but eventually she let herself appear to Antonia. They would embrace and dance, or become children again and play and laugh. They never talked about Jenny or men or life. They only played like children.

In the morning, Magali would rise up out of Antonia's body and float away, to wander again through the streets of Villa Rosario over by the Perequete River, searching for something.

Chapter Seventeen

It was a week later that don Fernando received a call from La Chorrera.

"Uncle, it's Jorge Manuel."

"Ah Koke, how are you?"

"Not good uncle, we have a burundanga death," Jorge Manuel said.

"What? Who is it?" don Fernando asked.

"A girl named Luna Delgada," said Jorge Manuel.

Don Fernando frowned. "Luna..." he asked, "a prostitute who works the streets near Calle del Puerto?"

"Yes! Uncle, how did you know?"

"That's the girl who told Jenny that the pimp Rodriguez was spreading rumors about the girl who died here," don Fernando said. "Tell me what happened."

"Her body was found several days ago in an alley, uncle. There were a few bruises on one arm but no major trauma. We didn't know what she died of, so I sent a blood sample to the Ministry of Justice's Forensic Laboratory in Panama City as you suggested. We just got the lab report this morning. She died from an overdose of burundanga."

"Were there any other drugs in her system?" don Fernando asked.

"Just a small amount of marijuana."

"Did you search her apartment?" don Fernando asked.

"Yes, uncle, the same day that we found the body and identified her. She lived with her parents in a small house on Calle V Este. We told her parents that we were looking for clues and they let us search, but we found no drugs there. But she actually worked out of another apartment—an apartment she shared with several other prostitutes. I don't think her parents knew what she did to make her money. A lot of young prostitutes get together and rent an apartment for that reason, you know... to hide their work from their parents. So we got a search warrant and searched that whole place. We found marijuana, but all those girls use marijuana. We never arrest them for that. But there were no other drugs there. "

"You interviewed her roommates?" don Fernando asked.

"Yes, they were all shocked and scared. We asked them about any boyfriends, enemies, recent clients... we asked if any colombianos had been hanging around recently. They said no. She didn't have a boyfriend, no enemies, and no recent weird clients."

"Hmmmm... you know, Koke, maybe I should bring Dani to La Chorrera and the three of us should talk. This is a bad case," don Fernando said, then he paused. "How long was Luna living with those other girls?"

"Over two years, uncle. They were all friends," Jorge Manuel replied.

"Hmmmm..." don Fernando said. "I remember Jenny told me that Luna worked the hotels in the neighborhood, but you know, Koke, most of the time when prostitutes stay in one place for a while, they build up a regular clientele. And often they keep records of the regulars and how much they pay, et cetera. Did you ask to see their records?"

"No, uncle, I did not think of that," Jorge Manuel replied.

"Well, let's do this, Koke: you go back and talk to those girls again and see if you can get their client list and any records they have. If they don't want to share those records, you tell them that we have information that they are in great danger and that we are trying to protect them. That should scare them into handing over any documents. I will get ahold of Dani and maybe we can meet in your office sometime tomorrow."

"Okay, uncle, thank you."

After don Fernando hung up, he sat and thought for a while. Panama was a victim of its own geography, he thought, being the isthmus that connected Colombia to Central and North America. Panama was simply the easiest route for moving drugs to the insatiable noses and veins of the North American gringos. Independent *portadores* would contract to hike the jungle trails through the porous and unguarded southern border of Panama with backpacks full of drugs. Sometimes, small groups of portadores would make the trek guarded by armed cartel members, moving through the jungle like small armies. For larger shipments, the Colombian cartels would hide the drugs inside legitimate cargo in shipping containers that were being shipped from the Colombian port of Cartagena to the bustling and chaotic port of Colón, Panama. From Colón, the drugs could be loaded onto speedboats or disguised fishing vessels for transport up the Atlantic side of Panama to Limón, Costa Rica. Or the drugs could be driven to Panama City and then placed on boats for transport up the Pacific side of Panama to any number of obscure jungle ports on the Osa Peninsula in Costa Rica. Or the cartels could hide the drugs in trucks and cars and ship the entire vehicle—even fleets of vehicles— from Cartagena to Colón and drive through Panama.

It all depended on where law enforcement was weakest. From Panama, the cartel had so many routes to choose from. Even with the help of the US coast guard, Panama couldn't patrol both the Atlantic and the Pacific sides at the same time. The cartels would simply pick the route each day that had the least surveillance. Already this year, the authorities had seized more than thirty tons of cocaine from boats or trucks. And that was probably only one percent of what was getting through. From Limón on the north coast of Costa

Rica, the cartels had an easy speedboat ride to Nicaragua or Honduras. From the southern Osa Peninsula of Costa Rica, the cartel could sail to either Nicaragua or El Salvador. Or they could simply drive their shipments through Panama, through Costa Rica, and into Nicaragua. Once they made it out of Costa Rica, there was simply no police surveillance, and they had no impediments until they got to the US border.

Don Fernando blamed the US for Panama's drug program. The cartels used to simply fly their drugs into Mexico. Those were drug-free days in Panama. But then the US started Operation *Eye in the Sky* and used the radar in their AWAC planes to monitor all small aircraft flying from Colombia into Mexico. Then they would simply radio in coordinates to the Mexican federal police, who then met the Colombian planes wherever they landed and arrested everyone on board. The program was so successful that the cartels simply stopped flying drugs into Mexico and starting moving them through Panama. The US should have foreseen that!

Ah, don Fernando thought, it was just as Dani always said: every problem that exists was the solution to a previous problem.

He looked at his watch. It was past noon. Dani should be up by now. Don Fernando picked up the phone and dialed Dan's number.

"Hola, Dani," he said when Dan answered. "It's Fernando... Yes, Dani, it is past morning, time to get up. Well, the reason I called is that I need your help. Another young girl has been killed by burundanga... Yes, I know. No, not here—in La Chorrera, a young prostitute named Luna... Luna Delgada. No, I don't know if she knew your Magali. Jenny knew her, but she did not work at Jenny's. You remember Jorge Manuel? Yes, yes, I know... you are still upset with him, but that was more than two years ago, Dani. Anyway, he just got the lab report this morning and is still interviewing the dead girl's roommates. I hope to know more by tomorrow. The reason I am calling, Dani, is that I would be very grateful if you would come with me tomorrow so that you and I and Jorge Manuel can meet and talk about this case. Yes, I know Dani, but I would consider it a special favor. I need to stop this disease from infecting my town... Please? Ah, thank you, Dani, you are a true friend. I will pick you up at noon tomorrow. We will make Jorge Manuel buy us lunch. Yes, thank you."

Don Fernando hung up and leaned back in his chair and stared at the old map of Villa Rosario on his wall. Yes, he thought, he needed to stop this disease before it became an epidemic.

Chapter Eighteen

That night, Magali was hovering over Antonia's bed when she felt Dan thinking about her. She didn't want to leave Antonia's room, but Dan's vibration was strong. She floated out of Antonia's apartment, across town and into Dan's apartment. He was sitting at his desk pouring something from a bottle into a glass measuring cup. Magali looked at the liquid. It was dark brown, and seemed to have leaves and twigs in it. Magali watched as Dan measured it carefully and held the cup up to inspect the level.

"Are you going to drink that?" Magali asked.

Dan turned around slowly and glanced at her. His eyes had a dreamy far-away look.

"I've already had one glass," he said. "I thought I needed another one. But since you're here, I guess I don't."

He poured the mixture carefully from the measuring cup back into the bottle and put a cork in it.

"I didn't know if you would come back to see me," he said.

"I've been spending time with Antonia," Magali said.

"Ahh yes," Dan nodded, "I had heard you two were close."

Magali looked at him, or rather, into him.

"What's wrong, Dan?" she asked.

Dan took a deep breath and said, "They murdered you, Magali. They killed you."

"Yes... well... I supposed they did," she answered.

"And now they've murdered another young woman, a woman named Luna Delgada from La Chorrera... did you know her?"

"No..." Magali said, "I didn't know any Luna. Who is

she?"

"She was a prostitute," Dan said. "They killed her the same way they killed you."

"Oh," said Magali. She paused a minute, and then asked, "And how was that? I mean, how did I die?"

"They poisoned you with scopolamine, Magali."

"Hmmm, okay... I don't know what that is," she said.

"Don Fernando calls it burundanga," Dan said.

"Okay... I don't know what that is either. But either way, it doesn't matter."

"It does matter, Magali," Dan said.

She looked at him. She could tell that he was feeling something. Humans only used emotions to feel things, she realized, as if that was the only thing emotions could do.

"It doesn't matter to me, Dan. Everything is different now—nothing matters," she said.

"It matters to me, Magali," Dan said, "I loved you." Tears started to stream down his face. Magali watched them slide from his eyes and work their way down his cheeks to his jaw line. Some of them fell to the floor.

"Yes," she said. "I remember love... it brings a lot of pain, doesn't it? But believe me, Dan, it doesn't matter now."

Her form began to shimmer. Dan was afraid she was going to disappear again.

"Magali," he said. "Magali, listen—tomorrow I have to go to La Chorrera and help the police... help them find the person who killed you. You've got to help me. The police have no clues. Do you remember who did this to you?... how they did it?... why they did it?"

Magali stopped shimmering and tried hard to think. "There was a man," she said. "I think I knew him. He had a lot of secrets, like an old clock... I came home and I remember opening my door... I felt something touch the back of my neck... I turned around and he was there... then everything spun around... I tried to go inside, and I fell down... and then I died. Then I heard your voice in the graveyard. That made me happy, to hear your voice."

"Oh Magali," Dan said quietly, still crying. "Why did he kill you?"

"I don't know... I remember, after I died, he went through my apartment looking for something... I remember I could see he had a lot of secrets, secrets I never knew before. It's odd, don't you think? I guess that's what people are—just a huge tangled knot of secrets. Some people are so knotted up they don't even know that they have secrets..."

"Were there other people, besides this one guy, Magali?" Dan asked.

"I don't know... maybe," she said. "What does it matter?"

"Because we have to find him before he kills again!"

"Why?" Magali asked. "What does it matter if he kills again?"

"Magali!" Dan exclaimed. "Life is important. It's not right to kill, to take someone's life."

"I don't know, Dan..." she said, "Maybe it's not so important... I mean, it seems important to you, I understand that now. But it really isn't important. We just all get absorbed back into the earth."

Dan looked at her. There was something in how she said that sentence that seemed to mean something different.

"What do you mean, Magali?" he asked.

"Well, I remember how Father Lopez always talked about going up to heaven when we die... but we don't. The pull is downward, not upward to heaven, but downward, into the earth... You think the earth is made of rocks and soil, but it's not. The earth is us, Dan."

"What do you mean?" he repeated.

"The souls of the dead, Dan. We are the earth... the rocks, the loam, the water, the dust, the water, the lava, the ash..." She gave a little laugh. "Planets are just dead people, Dan... trillions of trillions of compressed dead people, burning white hot in the center, hard as rocks on the outside. The earth pulls us down into her... well... when we're ready to go to her..."

Dan's head shook involuntarily. What Magali was saying made no sense to him. Her form began to shimmer again.

"Magali, wait—don't leave. I need your help. I need to know why they killed you."

"I don't know why," she answered.

She began to fade, to become almost transparent.

"Wait!" Dan cried. "One more question! How many people are involved?"

Her light grew brighter for a second. He could see that she was thinking.

"Two," she said. "The man left my apartment and went to see another man."

"Any more men?"

"No," she said. "Only two."

And then she was gone.

Dan sat for a minute, looking at the space where she was. Then he looked at the bottle of ayahuasca. He realized he was still crying. He got up and went to the cupboard where he kept the whiskey.

Chapter Nineteen

At noon the next day, don Fernando pulled his police car into a parking space in front of the La Chorrera police department. Dan sat in the passenger seat, feeling very hungover. He had managed to shave that morning, and to put on clean clothes, in order to look presentable... but he had sat quiet for the drive from Villa Rosario to La Chorrera. Don Fernando knew his friend well enough to simply let him be and not talk.

Jorge Manuel was waiting inside the police lobby when don Fernando and Dan walked in. Jorge Manuel greeted his uncle warmly and shook Dan's hand respectfully. He knew that Dan still had feelings about the death of a prisoner that had happened in one of Jorge Manuel's jail cells a few years ago, but don Fernando had always told him not to talk to Dan about it—to simply let time heal Dan's feelings. Besides, Jorge Manuel never wanted to offend his uncle's friend. Dan had helped them solve two murders in La Chorrera over the past two years, and Jorge Manuel did not want to lose such an important resource.

"Are you hungry?" Jorge Manuel asked don Fernando. "Do you want to get some lunch first before we talk?"

Don Fernando glanced quickly over at Dan. "Yes," he told his nephew. "I think that would be a good idea. Let's go eat and we can talk afterwards."

"Los Cuñados?" Jorge Manuel suggested, knowing it was don Fernando's favorite restaurant in La Chorrera.

"An excellent choice," said don Fernando.

"Let me get a few things," said Jorge Manuel, and went back to his office to grab a thick manila envelope. Then the three men went outside and climbed into Jorge Manuel's new police chief's car. Dan took the back seat without saying a word.

Don Fernando looked around the car's spacious interior. "Nice," he said. "New?"

"Sí, uncle, the city council approved it last month. I think they wanted a more professional appearance for the department. They are giving us new uniforms too, and are letting us hire more officers."

"Ah, yes," don Fernando said. "Well, your city is doing well. Lots of construction. If you're not careful, soon there will be nothing between La Chorrera and Panama City except condos."

"It's true, uncle. The gringos like it here because they are close to Panama City but we're still a quiet town."

"That will change if you get too many condos," don Fernando said. "Too much success will destroy the very peace and quiet that makes this city attractive."

Dan sat quietly during the ride and half-listened to the two men talk. His mind was still focusing on what Magali had said to him last night. He kept turning it over, trying to pull some meaning out of her words. But his head was still hurting from the combination of ayahuasca and whiskey. Maybe he would feel better after he ate.

When the three men entered Los Cuñados, Dan nodded hello to Miguel, the owner of the restaurant. Dan didn't know him well, but had met him before and knew he was a close friend of Ricardo's. Miguel automatically escorted the three men to the private room in the back. He knew that when the two police chiefs came to eat at his restaurant, it was always to talk business, and that required privacy.

As Miguel was seating the men, Dan whispered to him. "Can you do me a favor and bring me some coffee right away?"

Miguel nodded and waved a busboy over quickly.

Dan's coffee arrived while Miguel was handing out menus and describing the daily specials. Dan sipped at his coffee and did not open his menu until Miguel asked him for his order. Then Dan opened the menu and pointed to the first thing he saw. He was hungry but he didn't care what they brought—he would eat it.

Dan continued to drink coffee quietly while don Fernando and Jorge Manuel talked. Jorge Manuel stole a quick look at Dan. Dan seemed to have a far-away look in his eyes. But Jorge Manuel remembered how strange and distant this gringo could be, so he simply continued chatting with don Fernando. They chatted about their respective families, gossiped about relatives, and shared complaints about their jobs, complaints about traffic problems, and the eternal complaints about the federal government of Panama.

After their food arrived, the conversation between Jorge Manuel and don Fernando turned again to the explosion in condominium construction on the northeast side of town, the side closest to Panama City.

"Did you have a chance to visit any of the new communities, Koke?" don Fernando was asking, "to see who is actually buying these condominiums?"

"Yes, uncle, I walked through several of them—it is all retired gringos, mostly from the United States, some from Germany, a few from France. But almost all older people. And I compared our arrests over the past month by neighborhood, I could not find any significant increase in drug arrests in the condo neighborhoods. Burglaries were up, of course. But not drug use. I do not think there is any connection between these new residents and the burundanga deaths. All of the condo owners I saw were white, not colombiano."

For the first time Dan spoke up. "Those are just the tenants, not the owners," he blurted.

Jorge Manuel was taken back. "But they are living there."

Dan shrugged. "They're just renting. Look at the advertisements for these condos—they all offer one, two, three, five, sometimes ten year leases. And those lease prices are low enough to be affordable for gringos. The developers are filling these condos with renters, not with buyers."

"But they have the option to buy, don't they?" Jorge Manuel protested. "Isn't that what these gringos are doing? Renting for a while to see if they like it, before they buy?"

"No," Dan said. "I mean, that's what the ads suggest. But look at the actual sale prices of the condos—they're too high. It's cheaper to rent, and it's more logical, especially if you are an older retired couple from the states. Why should you buy? That's why these long-term lease prices are so low, so attractive. The developers want to fill these condos with people, but they don't really want to sell the condos."

"What do you mean, Dani?" don Fernando asked.

"Look, there's too much construction," Dan explained. "Too much money pouring in. Panama's not in great shape economically, yet millions and millions of dollars are suddenly being invested in real estate? All in the past two or three years? All in this area? And the sale prices of the condos are outrageously high. But the lease prices are affordable— not for Panamanians, but for retired gringos. It's because the cartels need a way to launder their money. They're buying land, developing it, building condos faster than they can sell them, in order to hide their money. You only see white people in these condos, because the Colombians don't want to live in tiny condos. They've got huge mansions in Colombia— but they want a place to park their money for about a decade. So they make it attractive for older white people to live there for ten years or so until they die. Ten years is the statute of limitations for money laundering, right? You watch—in ten or twelve years, there will be no more easy leases. The cartels will reset the price of these condos, and all these properties will really start to go on the market. It's brilliant, really. The Colombians are creating the demand by offering these cheap leases, filling these places up, cleaning up the titles and the money, so that after ten years all their drug money will be clean and legitimate, and they can sell the condos, collect their money without any questions asked, and move wherever they want." Dan shook his head. "Ever notice that none of these developments are inside the city limits of La Chorrera? They're all in unincorporated areas, like Vacamonte or Nuevo Arraijan... and why? Because there's no regulation there. No banking laws. They can buy property easy and build easy, and nobody is going to look too closely at where that money comes from."

Don Fernando and Jorge Manuel sat quietly, trying to absorb what Dan had just said.

"How... how do you know all this, señor?" Jorge Manuel finally asked.

Dan shrugged. "I don't know. It just seems obvious to me."

Don Fernando asked, "So you think the owners of these condominiums are colombianos?"

"I guarantee it, amigo," Dan said, and smiled for the first time.

"And you think they are connected with these burundanga murders?" don Fernando asked.

Dan frowned. "Oh no, well, not directly... they are probably cartel chiefs, higher-up bosses just wanting to protect their wealth. They've got too much cash on their hands... I remember one dealer back in L.A. telling me that the biggest problem in drug dealing wasn't selling the drugs, or avoiding the police—it was what to do with all the cash. These cartels are drowning in cash and have to spend it somewhere, invest it somewhere, clean it somehow... and construction has always been the best way to launder money, both in the United States and here... but no, I don't think these condos have anything to do with Magali's or Luna's death... I was just saying there's more than meets the eye with all this new construction... I was just reacting to what Jorge Manuel was saying about the condo residents... that's all. The two men you are looking for are not connected—at least not directly—with these condominiums."

Don Fernando stared at Dan and asked, "What two men?"

Dan picked up his fork and resumed eating. Between bites he said, "There are only two men involved in these deaths... I don't know what the connection is between Magali and this Luna girl—they didn't know each other—but one or both of the two men knew both girls. And it wasn't a random killing. The man who poisoned Magali searched her apartment before he left, but I don't know what he was looking for... Did this Luna still have her purse with her?"

Dan looked over at Jorge Manuel. Jorge Manuel nodded and said, "Yes, but the contents had been dumped out on the ground."

"Really?" Dan said.

"Yes, but it did not look as if anything was missing. Her cell phone was there, and there was some money—a few bills—left on the ground along with her personal items."

Dan continued, "Huh... Well, you might want to ask her roommates if there was anything else that Luna carried with her at night, a package, or a second handbag or something... Both girls had something these men wanted... but it wasn't drugs. Neither one of these girls were involved with drugs. Maybe they didn't even know what they had that was so valuable... maybe it was a secret, even to them... But, back to the drug angle... clearly these two men are involved in drugs. But I don't think they're cartel members... I think they're independents, operating on their own."

Don Fernando and Jorge Manuel just sat there silently, looking at Dan. Finally don Fernando asked, "How do you know all this, Dani?"

Dan paused. Maybe he had said too much. He certainly didn't want to reveal that he had been talking to Magali's ghost, nor did he want don Fernando to know that he was using ayahuasca again. He knew how his friend felt about that. He remembered how don Fernando had tricked him into rehab last year, and he didn't want to go through that again.

"Well, I could be wrong, don Fernando. It's just that my police experience and training tells me that there are two rogue killers involved. They're not professional. In fact, they are very sloppy. A professional cartel assassin would not have left so many fake clues—heroin *and* cocaine—on Magali's table. Hell, a professional would not have even left a body. Plus, these were innocent girls—the cartel would have no reason to kill them. So I conclude these are rogue killers, not connected to any cartel. And I say there are two of them, because my experience is that stupid killers work in pairs. Smart killers work alone, but stupid killers need to feed off each other to keep killing."

Jorge Manuel nodded. What Dan was saying seemed reasonable to him. Don Fernando wasn't so sure.

"And why do you believe that these two girls did not know each other?" he asked.

"Just a hunch," Dan said. "We have no evidence that says they did."

Don Fernando pursed his lips. He made a mental note to quiz Dan later in private.

Dan continued eating. There was a pause in the conversation. Then don Fernando pointed at the manila envelope by Jorge Manuel's side. "What did you bring, Koke?"

Jorge Manuel opened the envelope and spread the papers on the table, glad to be doing something useful. "This is the lab report on Luna Delgada. These are the client records that her two roommates gave me. This is the dead girl's calendar book."

Dan looked over at the papers. He picked up the lab report and held it to his nose. He thought he could almost smell the perfume of María José Vargas on the paper. It was a pleasant scent. He thumbed through the report, spotted the line about burundanga and marijuana, and put the report back on the table and returned to his food.

Don Fernando was reading through the records of the three prostitutes. There was a primitive type of ledger, showing the names of clients and the amounts they paid. There was a list of notes about activities each client preferred.

And there were several pages of notes showing expenses and how those costs were divided.

"Whoa!" exclaimed don Fernando.

"What is it?" asked Dan.

"Lucas Antigua Martin," don Fernando said.

"Who is that?" Dan asked.

"One of Luna's clients," don Fernando said, as he quickly rifled through the other pages of the client ledger. "And he was a regular client of hers."

"And?" Dan asked.

"He was a client of Magali's too," don Fernando explained.

Dan put down his fork and got up and went and stood behind don Fernando and looked at the report over don Fernando's shoulder.

"A pretty frequent client," Dan commented.

"Yes."

"How much was he spending a month?" Dan asked.

Don Fernando flipped through the pages. "Shit, Dani, over five hundred dollars a month! He doesn't make that kind of money. He repairs trucks for a living. Plus he was spending money at Jenny's too."

"Hmmm, can I see that report, don Fernando?" Dan asked.

Dan quickly flipped through the pages and then handed the report back to don Fernando and then went back to his seat.

Don Fernando looked through the pages again. "This makes no sense, Dani," don Fernando said. "I know this Lucas. He is as simple and dumb as they come. He can barely count to ten."

"Secrets within secrets," Dan said.

Don Fernando looked at Dan quizzically.

"Maybe he has a secret side," Dan explained. "You say he repairs trucks?"

"Yes," don Fernando said, "he runs a small truck repair shop on the east side of Villa Rosario, near the Perequete River. They sell tires, do small repairs, nothing too complicated, more like a junk yard than a business."

"Hmmm, really? Maybe the just the sort of place to unload drugs from trucks," Dan suggested. "An out-of-the-way workshop with tools and stupid workers who like to get paid in cash... Might be worthwhile to put the place under surveillance—see what kind of truck traffic they actually get."

Don Fernando nodded his head yes. "That's a good idea."

"Look at this," Jorge Manuel said. He had been looking through Luna's calendar book while Dan and don Fernando were talking.

"What is it?" don Fernando said.

"This journal has a calendar on the right hand page and a to-do list on the left hand side. I didn't see this before because I was only looking at the pages before her death, to see if she was meeting someone. But look here—she wrote 'H—airport' on next month's calendar, on the third. Maybe she was supposed to take that fellow Hernán to the Tocumen Airport in Panama City."

Dan and don Fernando looked at the calendar where Jorge Manuel was pointing.

"Does she have a car?" don Fernando asked.

"I don't know," admitted Jorge Manuel. "But I will find out."

"Or maybe she was going to meet him at the airport," Dan suggested. He looked at don Fernando and asked, "Is there any way we can screen the names of all the passengers flying in and out of Tocumen Airport for the name Hernán?"

"I think we could," don Fernando said. "We have enough lead time..." And then he mused aloud, "Assuming it's the Tocumen Airport... maybe it's a different airport... maybe it's a private plane. This country is dotted with private landing strips."

"True," said Jorge Manuel. "The narcotráficos will just use any flat field."

Don Fernando and Jorge Manuel continued to look

through the documents. Dan simply stared off into space. After a few minutes, he turned to don Fernando and said, "Let me ask a stupid question, don Fernando... about this guy Lucas... does he, by any chance, have anything to do... with clocks?"

"Clocks?"

"Yeah, you know, alarm clocks, cuckoo clocks, grandfather clocks...?"

Don Fernando shook his head. "Not that I know of Dani. Why?"

Dan shrugged and said, "I don't know—just a random question."

"The dead girl had a tattoo of a clock," Jorge Manuel said softly.

"What?" both don Fernando and Dan said at the same time.

"I didn't bring the photos of the body with me," Jorge Manuel said. "I have them back at the office. But on her shoulder was a tattoo of a clock face. She had a couple of other tattoos, but I remember this one because it was unique—the clock had no hands... you know what I mean? It was the clock face, like a watch, but there was no hour hand and no minute hand."

"I'd like to see that," Dan said.

"Of course. If we are finished here, we can go there now," Jorge Manuel said.

"Maybe in a minute," Dan said. Let me ask a few more questions. Where was this girl Luna's body found exactly?"

"In an alley about seven blocks from the apartment she shared with her two roommates," Jorge Manuel answered.

"Was this near the hotels she worked, her route so to speak?"

"Sí, Señor Dan. It was three blocks from one of her regular hotels, the Hierba Hotel. She would hang out in the hotel bar. The hotel staff knew her, worked with her. If a hotel guest picked her up, she would pay a percentage to the hotel. If someone else picked her up, she would make them get a room in that hotel, and the hotel would pay her a percentage... it's a common arrangement between many streetwalkers and hotels here."

"And did anyone at the hotel see her the night before her body was found?"

"They said she came into the bar around eight, but didn't stay. She ordered a beer, but didn't finish it. Left alone."

"Did she get a phone call?"

"We think not. Her phone was in her purse when her body was found the next morning. There were several unanswered texts from her roommates asking why she hadn't come back to the apartment, but no completed phone calls after seven the night before."

"Hmmm," Dan frowned. "Maybe she saw someone... Can you have your men interview the staff and regulars in that bar again? Something must have made her leave the bar... Oh, and ask them if she was carrying anything. It might be something small... Maybe someone saw her carrying something that was missing when her body was found."

"Of course, Señor Dan," Jorge Manuel said.

Dan sat and thought for a minute, then frowned and turned to don Fernando. "I can't connect the dots, don Fernando. We've still got no real clues... Let's go look at the picture of this tattoo... and maybe before we leave La Chorrera, we could go and talk with Jenny... We may have to start back at square one... None of this makes any sense."

Chapter Twenty

At the same time that Dan and the two police chiefs were leaving the El Restaurante de Los Cuñados and driving over to Jorge Manuel's office in La Chorrera, Magali was drifting through a run-down industrial area near the Perequete River in Villa Rosario. She floated along a dirt road that was lined with abandoned shacks. Nobody seemed to live on this road. Around the bend she saw an old garage with tin metal sides. The front doors were open, and noise was coming from within. She floated over to the building and drifted through the walls to the inside. She saw two men working on a large truck. One man was inside the cab of the truck, crouched over. He seemed to be removing pieces of the floorboards, and handing them to a tall skinny man standing outside the truck.

Magali looked at the skinny man. His skin was like dark chocolate. He had a thin aquiline nose and thin lips. Magali thought his face was hard, cruel. She did not recognize him—she had never seen him before, either in Villa Rosario or at Jenny's.

The other man was still crouched over inside the truck, and Magali couldn't see his face. But she could tell he was short and stocky. Then she heard him grunt, and watched as he backed out of the cab, holding a package. When he turned around and handed it to the tall skinny man, Magali could finally see his face. All of a sudden, the currents that had been swirling around her and pulling her along, simply stopped. This man she recognized. This was the man who had come up behind her the last night she was alive. This was why the currents had been carrying her for the past week. This was the man she had been searching for...

Chapter Twenty-One

In the La Chorrera police station, Jorge Manuel carefully laid out twenty large color photographs across the conference room table. Half of the photos were of the crime scene itself. The other ten photos were of Luna's body in the morgue.

The images of Luna sprawled out on the earthen ground of the alley like a discarded piece of trash made Dan both angry and a little queasy. Luna appeared to be no older than 22 or 23 years old. She was dressed in a typical Panamanian streetwalker outfit: high heels, a too-tight short dress, and sleeveless top.

Truth be known, Dan had seen more death over the past decade in Panama than he ever had working as a detective in Los Angeles. Back in L.A., he had mostly worked white collar crime, not violent crime. He tried to act unaffected in front of the other two men, but it was hard to look at the photographs that showed Luna's lifeless face.

He picked up the close-up photo of the clock tattoo. It was as Jorge Manuel had described it: a clock or stopwatch face with no hands. It held no significance for Dan.

Nonetheless, he asked Jorge Manuel, "Can you have your men ask around the tattoo shops in town? See if they can identify who did the tattoo, when, and especially if Luna was with anyone when it was done?"

"Sí, señor."

Dan looked closer at the photograph and said, "See how there is a faint redness around these blue lines? It looks to be a recent tattoo, just a few weeks old. Whoever did it should remember it."

Jorge Manuel peered at the photo and nodded his

head in agreement.

Dan looked through the other photos. He picked up a close-up photo of Luna's left arm. It showed some bruises on the inside of her left bicep.

"Do you have a magnifying glass?" he asked Jorge Manuel.

Jorge Manuel got a large magnifying glass from a side table and handed it to Dan. Dan studied the bruise marks.

"Look at these three marks," Dan said, "how the middle one is slightly further away from the other two. They look like pressure marks from fingertips where someone grabbed her arm, but the marks are backwards. If a right handed man grabbed her from the front, he would be grabbing her left arm, and his fingers would be pressing against the inside of her arm like this, but his middle finger would be more towards him, because it's longer. But this bruise—and I think this is the middle finger here—this bruise is away from him. And if a left handed man grabbed her arm hard from the front, the bruises would be on her right arm. This bruise looks like someone grabbed her hard from behind with his left hand, so that his fingers made this pattern,"—Dan pointed at the bruise—"so his middle finger was more towards her back. See that?"

Both don Fernando and Jorge Manuel nodded yes.

"So you think the killer was left-handed?" Jorge Manuel asked.

"No, I think he was right handed. He grabbed her from behind, using his left hand to grab her left arm, to hold her still, because his right hand was holding some kind of vial or bottle of burundanga powder, which he poured down the back of her neck."

Don Fernando looked at Dan quizzically.

"That's how he is administering the powder," Dan explained. "He is pouring it down the back of their blouses. That way it lessens the chance that some of it will blow back on him."

Don Fernando looked at the photo of the bruises

and frowned. Dan bit his lip. He couldn't tell don Fernando what Magali had said about feeling something touch the back of her neck when she came home that night, so he just shrugged and said, "It's just a theory, don Fernando."

Don Fernando nodded.

"Where is Luna's body now?" Dan asked Jorge Manuel.

"In the cemetery," Jorge Manuel said. "The funeral was two days ago."

"Hmm. Okay," Dan said. He leaned back and thought for a minute. He was about to advise Jorge Manuel to have his evidence technician take impressions of the back of the next victim's neck with adhesive tape, to see if there were remnants of burundanga powder on the back of their necks, to confirm the method of poison delivery. But then he realized that he was assuming there were going to be more bodies. He tried to analyze why he felt that way, and he realized again that he was completely in the dark about the motive for these two killings. If he knew the motive, then he could predict if there were going to be more killings. But all he had was a bad feeling, a bad feeling that in fact there were going to be more murders. But why? Why did he feel that way? Something in what Magali had said... what was it? She had asked, *"What does it matter if he kills again?"* It was the way she had said that, Dan thought, like she knew he was going to kill again. Shit.

"Listen, Jorge Manuel," he spoke quietly, "if any more bodies turn up, have your technicians use a piece of adhesive tape on the back of their necks, to see if you can lift off any burundanga powder, you know, like they lift fingerprints... but make sure they wear gloves."

Jorge Manuel nodded his head.

"Come on don Fernando, let's go visit Jenny. I've seen enough of these pictures," Dan said, and stood up.

*   *   *

In the car, on the way over to Jenny's, don Fernando

couldn't stand it any longer.

"Dani," he said, "I didn't want to ask you in front of Jorge Manuel, but I have to know—are you drinking that brujo juice again?"

Dan gave a little laugh. "You mean whiskey? Yeah, I've been hitting that every night."

"You know what I mean, Dani," don Fernando said sternly.

"Oh *that* brujo juice," Dan laughed again. "No, not really. Occasionally I take a bottle out and open it, just to smell it, you know, for old time's sake. But no, I am not indulging in that stuff again."

Don Fernando pursed his lips and shook his head. He knew his friend was lying.

"Be careful Dani. That stuff is dangerous."

"I will be, don Fernando. It's just that this case is... personal, you know?"

"Sí, amigo, I understand."

They rode the rest of the way to Jenny's neighborhood in silence, each man wrapped in his own thoughts.

*   *   *

Don Fernando parked his police car several blocks away from Jenny's brothel. He turned the engine off and checked his watch. He knew that it was way too early for the brothel to be open, but he also knew Jenny's habitual schedule. She would be there, going over the books from the night before, and making sure the rooms were ready for later tonight. He pulled out his cell phone and dialed her private number.

"Hola, Jenny," he said. "It's Fernando. ¿Cómo estás? Bueno. Listen, Dan and I are parked about three blocks away. Can we stop in for just a few minutes to ask you some questions? Thank you. We'll be right there."

The two men got out of the car and walked the three blocks. Jenny was waiting for them at the door. She led them

105

into the front living room.

As they sat down, she simply looked at the two men, with one eyebrow raised, and waited for them to speak.

"You heard that the girl Luna was found dead?" don Fernando asked.

Jenny nodded her head and only said, "Yes... very sad."

Dan spoke up. "Jenny, if we may speak honestly... and confidentially... this can't leave this room..." He paused while Jenny nodded her agreement.

"We are stymied with this case, Jenny. Both Magali and Luna were murdered."

Jenny's face darkened. Dan paused again to let Jenny digest that sentence.

"And both were poisoned in the same way, Jenny, and probably by the same person. But we have no clue why. These two girls didn't know each other. Neither of them were involved in anything illegal. The only thing they had in common was their profession, and the fact that they both knew Lucas Antigua Martin..."

"Really?" Jenny said and looked even more concerned. "He came by the other night, asking if Antonia was back."

"Oh?" Dan said, "And is she?"

"No, and frankly I'm worried about her. She refuses to leave her apartment in Villa Rosario. My girls have been taking turns bringing her food. I went to see her yesterday, and she looks awful. She's lost a lot of weight, and looks pale and sickly. She acts like she has *la mordida de murciélago*," Jenny said.

Dan glanced at don Fernando. He didn't know what this Spanish slang meant.

"A bat bite," don Fernando explained, "as if she had been bitten by a vampire... she looks as if she was losing her soul."

Dan nodded and frowned. "What's wrong with her?" he asked.

"She's is mourning, but it's consuming her," Jenny said. "I did not realize how much she loved Magali."

"And how does this Lucas guy know her?" Dan asked.

Jenny shrugged. "The same way everyone knows my girls, señor."

"No, I meant... what's his relationship with her? Does he know her outside of here?"

"No," Jenny said. "He met her here the same way he met Magali."

Don Fernando spoke up. "How often does Lucas come here, Jenny?"

"Well, that is interesting you should ask that, Fernando," Jenny said. "He used to come by a five or six times a year, but about three months ago, he started coming by once a week."

"Once a week?" don Fernando exclaimed and shook his head. "Jenny, he was spending more than five hundred a month on Luna, and I guarantee your girls charge more than Luna did."

"As you know, don Fernando, I never discuss money with my visitors," Jenny said flatly. "I merely provide introductions, nothing more."

"Of course," don Fernando said. "I understand."

"You said he was here the other night?" Dan asked. "Who did he see?"

"No one," Jenny answered. "He never even stepped inside. He just came to the door and asked about Antonia, and when I told him she wasn't here, he just nodded and left."

"Was he attached to her?" Dan asked. "Was she, like... a favorite of his?"

"No, not really. He had only been with her one time before."

"And what is your impression of him?" Dan asked.

"He does not leave much of an impression... He is quiet, but heavy, like a bag of potatoes."

Don Fernando grunted in agreement. He thought that was a good description of Lucas.

"Is he shy?" Dan asked.

"No," Jenny said. "He is just stupid."

Dan leaned back and thought about this. He certainly could understand a man getting attached to a particular prostitute—after all, both he and Ricardo had become attached to Magali. And certainly there had been times when Magali had been busy, and Dan simply went home without seeing anyone else. But this Lucas was not in that category. He had only been with Antonia one previous time—too little time to form an attachment. And clearly he liked sex— between Luna and Jenny's, he was seeing hookers as often as twice a week. So he must have shown up at Jenny's the other night for some other reason than sex. He must have wanted specifically to see Antonia. Otherwise, he would have stayed and seen another girl. Dan had a bad feeling about this Lucas guy. Stupid or not, he might be a murderer.

"Don Fernando," Dan suddenly said, "we need to go see Antonia now. She may be in danger.

"Let me draw you a little map," Jenny said. "She lives on one of those streets without names or numbers."

Jenny got up and got a piece of paper from a drawer and drew a quick map for don Fernando. Unmarked addresses were common in most Panamanian towns, and Dan was hoping that gave Antonia some security. Hopefully that's why Lucas had to come to Jenny's to look for Antonia— because he didn't know where she lived.

Chapter Twenty-Two

It was a good thing that Jenny had drawn a map for don Fernando and Dan, because they never would have found Antonia's apartment without it. They had to squeeze their way through a two-foot gap between two buildings that Jenny had described as a tiny alley. That passageway led to a shaded courtyard in front of a small house that had been converted into four apartments. Dan and don Fernando climbed the stairway and knocked on Antonia's door.

Dan knew who Antonia was. He had never slept with her at Jenny's, but he had seen her walking in Villa Rosario with Magali. Ricardo had spoken of her and, of course, he had seen her at Magali's funeral. But the pale creature who opened the door after they knocked a second time did not resemble the Antonia he remembered. The Antonia he remembered was thin, but this girl was at least twenty pounds thinner—almost skin and bones. There were dark circles under her eyes, and her skin had a grayish tone that reminded him of Luna's lifeless face in the morgue photographs.

"Hello, Antonia," Dan said. "My name is Dan Landes. I'm a friend of Ricardo's and I was a close friend of Magali's. This is don Fernando, the police chief in town."

Antonia's face showed no reaction, but after a moment she said, "I know who both of you are."

"Jenny drew us a map to get to your house," Dan continued. "We're investigating the... the circumstances around Magali's death. We just want to ask you some questions about people she knew."

Antonia just stood there and stared into space, as if she hadn't heard a word he had said.

Dan decided to take a chance. He reached out and lightly touched Antonia's arm. The skin felt cold.

"Antonia," he said, "I know Magali comes to see you. She told me."

Slowly, Antonia turned and looked directly at Dan for the first time.

"You've seen her too?" she asked.

"Yes, she has come to me twice since she died."

Antonia lowered her head and said softly, "She comes to me every night."

Dan let his hand press more firmly on Antonia's arm.

"Antonia, listen," he said, "Magali was murdered. Someone killed her. We're trying to catch this man. Can we come in and talk with you, just for a few minutes?"

Antonia nodded her head yes, and stepped back to let them enter. Don Fernando followed Dan into the apartment with his head lowered. What Dan had said to Antonia confirmed don Fernando's fears—Dan had been using ayahuasca again. It was the only way that he could be talking with the dead.

Things were out of his hands now.

Antonia sat down in a wooden chair and gestured towards a large sofa for the two men to sit on.

Dan glanced at don Fernando. The cat's head was out of the bag, Dan thought, so he might as well let it all out. "Listen Antonia," he said, "the night that Magali was killed, she was unlocking the front door to her apartment when a man came up behind her—someone she knew. And a minute later she was dead. We think this man might have been Lucas Antigua Martin. Do you know him?"

Antonia shook her head slowly no. "I do not recognize that name, señor," she said.

"Jenny said he was a client of yours one time recently," Dan said.

Antonia shrugged. "I sleep with many men, señor. I do not remember their names."

Don Fernando spoke up. "He's a short, fat man, bald...

with small beady eyes, doesn't talk too much, seems stupid... well actually, he is stupid... and probably had dirty hands because he works on trucks."

"Ah, yes. I remember him—he was gross," Antonia said. "I remember him because I asked him why he couldn't finish paying for his tattoo if he had all that new money, and he got mad and said it *was* finished."

Dan involuntarily took a breath in. "It was a tattoo of a clock, wasn't it?" he said.

"Yes, but it wasn't finished," she said.

"Because it had no hands," Dan said.

Antonia nodded yes.

"And what did you mean all that *new* money?" he asked

"He paid me in brand new twenty dollar bills. He told me he had a rich uncle in the United States."

Dan leaned back in the sofa and closed his eyes and thought: new money... new money... What if he had been barking up the wrong tree all this time? What if this case had nothing to do with drugs?

"Antonia," he suddenly said, "do you still have any of those twenty dollar bills that Lucas gave you?"

His voice seemed to startle Antonia, but she nodded, and said, "Maybe," and got up and went into her bedroom. A minute later she returned holding three twenty-dollar bills, and held them out to Dan. He selected one and looked at it.

It was brand new. It had that crisp sticky new money feel to it. Dan squinted and looked at the tiny lines along the border—they were precise and distinct. He ran his finger along the lines of Andrew Jackson's coat—it had the proper raising printing. He looked at directly at the color of the number 20 on the lower right hand side of the bill—it had the proper copper color. He shifted the bill and looked at the same number 20 and watched it change to green—it had the proper color-changing ink. He held it up to the light and found the watermark of Jackson's face on the right hand side of the bill. He found the security thread on the left hand side of the bill. He wished he had a magnifying glass—his eyes weren't good enough to read the writing in the security thread. He closed his eyes and rubbed the bill with his fingers for several minutes, just trying to get a feel for the bill—some type of sensation, some type of intuition...

When he opened his eyes, he saw that both don Fernando and Antonia were watching him. He smiled at them both and then asked Antonia, "Could I see the other two bills?"

She handed them to him. They were also crisp. He folded all three bills and stuck them in his shirt pocket. Then he took out his wallet and pulled out three twenties and handed those bills to Antonia, saying, "I'll buy those from you."

Then he took a long look at Antonia's face. He understood why Jenny had said Antonia looked like she had been bitten by vampire.

"Antonia," he said, "I'm going to try and talk with Magali tonight. I'm going to ask her not to visit you anymore. She is... I don't know how to explain this... she is using your energy to allow her to stay here longer... she's feeding off you, and that's dangerous for you."

He turned to don Fernando and asked, "Is there any way you could post a police car in front of that alley tonight?"

Don Fernando frowned but nodded yes.

Dan turned back to Antonia and said, "Try and eat some of the food that Jenny's girls are bringing you. Try and get some rest tonight. We will come back in a few days and check on how you are doing. We may have more questions then... or we maybe some answers."

Antonia nodded. Dan stood up and turned towards the door. Don Fernando realized that Dan was leaving, so he stood up as well and followed Dan out the door and down the stairway.

"Let's go to your office," Dan said as they squeezed

through the tiny alleyway, "and I'll try and explain what I think is going on."

"Yes, please," don Fernando said, "I would appreciate that very much."

Chapter Twenty-Three

It was dark. Don Fernando drove back to the Villa Rosario police station in silence. Dan sat in the passenger side, lost in thought. But after they got inside don Fernando's office and he had closed the door, don Fernando couldn't hold back anymore.

"Dani, you told me you weren't drinking that brujo juice anymore! You know that stuff can make you crazy!"

Dan looked at don Fernando, smiled, but said coldly, "Mi amigo, I don't need to drink ayahuasca to talk to the dead. I could summon Magali to appear right here, right now, in your office. Would you like me to do that for you?"

Don Fernando stared at Dan. He could never tell whether Dan was serious or not, but he did not want to find out. Over the years, don Fernando had seen the strange things that brujos could do. Dan had been his friend for over ten years. But ever since Dan had started indulging in ayahuasca, he had become capable of scaring don Fernando.

Dan reached into his shirt pocket and took out the three twenty dollar bills he had bought from Antonia and looked at them again.

"I don't suppose you have a machine here for detecting magnetic ink?" he asked don Fernando.

Don Fernando snorted. "Dani, we barely have pens with regular ink."

"Do they have one in the police laboratory in Panama City?" Dan asked.

"I am sure they do."

"Well then," Dan said as he handed the bills to don Fernando, "can you send these to the laboratory there? I'm thinking these are counterfeit,"

Don Fernando looked at the bills closely, turning each one over in his hands.

"They look real, Dani," he said.

"I know, and that worries me. If they are counterfeit, then they are very, very good counterfeits. I could be wrong, but..." Dan's voice trailed off.

"But what?" don Fernando asked.

"Well, whoever killed Magali was after something. After he killed her, he searched her apartment. Magali told me he was looking for something. Magali knew this guy, but I don't think she knew him well. She didn't tell me his name... and I think that's because she didn't know his name. And then Jenny tells us that this guy Lucas Antigua Martin shows up looking for Antonia... and it kind of feels like the same deal. Antonia didn't know his name because she had only met him once before, but he had paid her with these brand new bills... and now suddenly he shows up looking for her... he doesn't want to see anyone else—just her... so maybe he didn't want to see her for sex, don Fernando... maybe it had something to do with this money... Maybe he wants his bills back... Maybe that's what he was searching for at Magali's apartment... maybe he was searching for the money that he had paid her with... and maybe that's why Luna died, too... maybe this Lucas guy paid her in brand new bills as well... and he's trying to cover his tracks, or get rid of witnesses, or maybe just get his bills back... maybe there's something about those bills that makes them valuable to this Lucas guy, so valuable he has to kill for them.

Don Fernando was nodding his head as he listened to Dan, but he was also frowning.

"What you say makes sense Dani, but I can't reconcile it being Lucas... I have known him all my life. He's like Jenny said—a sack of potatoes, just as dull and stupid as they come. Maybe it's somebody else?"

"Maybe," Dan said, "That's very possible. Maybe someone else, or some other group, is just using his shop as a place to print the bills and just paying him off in new money. He could just be a patsy—I don't know—but he's the only one we know of so far that knew Magali and Luna and Antonia."

Don Fernando nodded and walked over to his desk and sat down, opened the drawer, and took out a large magnifying glass, and started studying one of the bills.

After a few minutes, he put down the magnifying glass. "They look legitimate to me, Dani, but I'll call María José Vargas at the lab first thing in the morning and have these taken over to her."

"And can you put surveillance on this Lucas guy?" Dan asked.

"Hmmm... I think what I'll do is have my men check out his shop first thing in the morning. If there are other people there, we'll just watch. But if he's the only one there, I think I'm just going to arrest him, Dani, and have a little chat with him in the back room of the jail."

Dan had heard stories about the back room at the jail. "Well, I'll leave that up to you, don Fernando." Dan checked his watch. It was late.

"I've got to go now, don Fernando. I'll check with you in the morning."

"Where are you going, Dani?"

"I'm going to go have a chat with Magali," he said, and walked out the door.

Don Fernando watched him leave, sighed, shook his head, and picked up the magnifying glass again.

Chapter Twenty-Four

Dan left don Fernando's office and headed back to his apartment. Luckily, the moon was shining bright. There were no street lights in Villa Rosario, and the broken sidewalks were treacherous to walk at night without moonlight to illuminate the way. Dan hurried along, stepping carefully. He knew he had all the ingredients to assemble the ayahuasca mixture waiting for him in his apartment, but the process of preparing the final potion would take him another two hours.

At the same time that Dan was getting to his apartment, Father Lopez was well into his second bottle of wine. He normally would crawl into bed after the first bottle, but for some reason tonight, the wine was not doing its usual job of numbing his turning thoughts.

Father Lopez was not the kind of man given to morbid thoughts, but tonight morbid thoughts had found him. He felt old. His body ached every time he moved. There was no fluidity to his movements. He no longer recognized the pale and cadaverous skull that looked back at him in the mirror. Breathing was no longer an easy, unconscious, and automatic event, to be taken for granted. Except for wine, food had lost much of its appeal. He just felt very, very old. And when one feels old, the mind turns to thoughts of death. And when one thinks of death, it is natural to weigh and measure the quality of what has passed for one's life. And so it was for Father Lopez on this night. He had maneuvered himself into the large easy chair after the first bottle of wine, knowing he would probably sleep there tonight once he had opened the second bottle of wine. No point in risking a fall on the way to the bed.

He was leaning back in the chair, sipping on the wine, and resting the glass on his chest between sips, while his thoughts took their own pathway through dark speculations and darker memories. He wondered how he would die. He hoped he would simply slip away in his sleep, unconscious and unaware of death. But he knew this is rarely the case. He had sat vigil at too many of his own parishioners' deathbeds to innocently believe that death is quiet and gentle. It was usually, if not always, horrible and painful. The old parishioners of his church almost always went gasping for air—air that could not get in—and they slowly suffocated, with a horrible look in their eyes. If there was any relief in death, it was that it removed that horror from their eyes.

He thought of his Savior, dying on the cross, how painful that must have been. He knew that crucifixion kills by suffocation—that the victim, unable to rest or move, all his weight suspended, eventually, after so many hours, has to let his head fall forward, unable to hold it up, and the weight of the head and body on the chest makes it impossible to breathe, and the victim slowly suffocates. And so it is for all of us, he thought—we all die by crucifixion.

There was a time, many decades ago, when the thought of Jesus dying on the cross filled Father Lopez with determination to do good in the world, to lead an exemplary Christian life, to inspire others. But those ambitions had been eroded away by time... by time, external circumstances, and his own sins.

He took another sip of wine. He did not want to revisit his sins, but his thoughts had a mind of their own... He remembered that time, years ago, when he and don Fernando had gotten together and decided to kill an evil brujo who lived outside of town. They plotted how to sneak up to his wooden shack in the mountains, trap him there, and kill him. He remembered how he had built a bonfire in a pit by the side of that man's broken-down hovel, and how they had thrown his body into the fire of burning wood and trash, and watched him burn to death, twisting in the flames.

The image of that man's blackened face screaming in pain haunted Father Lopez for years. He knew it had to be done, because that brujo had been preying on the young people of the town, kidnapping them, stealing their souls, enslaving their bodies, then killing them and burying their bodies up in the mountains. He and don Fernando had decided the brujo had to be eliminated—that it had to be done to protect the community... but still... over the years Father Lopez had wondered whether killing that brujo was any different than the Roman soldiers killing Jesus to protect their community. They probably saw Jesus as a brujo, a supernatural being, capable of bringing the dead to life, threatening to convert the young people to his ways, threatening to destroy their community, their laws, and their way of life. They too probably felt they had no other option than to kill Jesus.

He thought of the crimes he had gained knowledge of over the years as he had listened to his parishioners' confessions... murders, rapes, thefts, betrayals... all the crimes he had done nothing about because of the sacred oath of confessional confidentiality. Was he any less complicit than his parishioners? Didn't his silence make him a co-conspirator? Equally as guilty? Or worse, what about the times he had told don Fernando about the crimes, helping don Fernando entrap the parishioner through some investigative pretext that never would have happened had Father Lopez not broken his sacred oath? To be a priest who heard confession was to be damned—damned if you did nothing, and damned if you acted. Who created this ritual— this ritual of absolution? Why should the sinner be absolved of guilt for his actions? Why shouldn't they suffer guilt and shame? No one absolved Father Lopez of his actions—he had to suffer with his memories.

He thought of Magali, and the abortion he had induced in her. He had no idea at that time how their paths would cross again that one night so many years later, after she had started working at Jenny's, after he had helped don Fernando kill the brujo, after he had started drinking every day... those days, those dark days when his faith had started to leave him... how lonely and destitute he had become... he had no one to give him absolution... only the wine... the blood of his Savior... that thin red narcotic... but even that nepenthe had stopped working... and those nights came more and more when he felt he could not go on... his life had become a fraud... he could barely get through the daily services in the church... he no longer wanted to be a priest... but there was nothing else he could do... he couldn't quit... he had no money, nowhere to live, nowhere to go, no other skills by which to earn a living, and by then he was no longer a young man. If he had quit, he would lose the guaranteed care of the church in his old age. What a racket the priesthood was—once the young idealistic men joined the seminary and were ordained, they were trapped, enslaved in an economic system from which there was no escape. Father Lopez had written the Bishop and asked for a transfer to another parish, hoping a change—any change— would save him. But the Bishop had refused, saying that Father Lopez was too important to Villa Rosario to relocate him. That refusal had doomed him to spend his remaining years as a complete fraud, a fake, a sham, an utterly lost soul.

Father Lopez took another sip of wine. It was Magali who had saved him. That night, so many years ago, when he had gotten drunk and wandered out of his quarters sometime after midnight, and somehow had stumbled unseen over to the park, where he sat on one of the benches, alone in the dark, while all his parishioners were home in their beds, fast asleep, undisturbed by their absolved sins. Magali must have been coming home from Jenny's that night, Father Lopez had always thought... she must have been cutting through the park on her way to her apartment... when she found him... found him sitting alone, drunk on that bench, his cheeks wet with tears. Bless her, bless her sweet prostitute heart, she had realized he was drunk. Without a word, she took him by the arm and hoisted him up on his feet, and walked him back to the church. He was amazed at how much strength was in that tiny body. He leaned on her while they walked, and she got him across the street, over to the back of the church, up the back staircase, safely back into his apartment, and guided him over to his bed, when she made him lie down.

He had never understood what had happened next, how it unfolded, who had done what, why it happened... he only knew that it did happen... it had not been a dream... and somehow the touch of her soft body had done what the church could not do, what all the wine in the world could not do... it had saved him. He awoke the next morning, naked in bed. She was gone.

In the years since that night, he had come to the conclusion that the gift that Magali had given him was a gift from God. It was unfathomable. It made no rational sense. It could not be understood. But it was an act of grace. He could never explain it, but he knew in his heart that God had given him a reprieve on life through Magali. God must have been there, in her body, that night, giving her body—the body of Christ—to him. And he had taken that body, and that body had taken him, and he had been swept away.

He had often wondered if Magali was Christ, come back in human form, like those unknown bodhisattvas that he had read about in Buddhism, that come back in human form out of compassion, to save suffering beings. For she had saved him that night... as she had saved hundreds of other men, by giving them her body to consume, to ease their suffering. He never understood how that act had saved him—how he could be saved and redeemed by something that would be universally condemned as a sin—but he had been saved, and somehow not being able to understand it made him realize the indefinable and unfathomable mystery of God.

He saw her in church a few weeks later. They never spoke of that night. Over the years, when they passed on the street, they would both just nod to each other and continue.

Bless her, bless her. It always filled his heart with joy to see her.

Father Lopez placed the half-empty glass of wine on the table next to him, leaned his head back against a pillow above the backrest of his easy chair, and fell asleep.

Chapter Twenty-Five

Dan's ayahuasca mixture was finally ready. He poured the brown liquid through a small strainer into a mason jar to screen out the leaves, stems, sticks, and any bugs that might have been attached to the various plants that made up his recipe. The process of preparing ayahuasca always put Dan into a type of trance, almost a religious reverie. It would bring back memories of how, some forty years ago, he had first experimented with ayahuasca, or *yage* as it was called back then, on a hippie trip to Central America, when he and another equally stupid college friend had flown to Panama on a quest to seek psychedelic plants. How young and dim-witted he had been back then. He was lucky to have survived that experience. His friend had not been so lucky. As a result, Dan had returned to the United States and sworn off all drugs, eventually joining the Los Angeles police force where he ended up working in the Crenshaw District. But then, decades later, after he had retired to Panama, circumstances conspired to bring ayahuasca back into his life, and he had accepted his fate as an ayahuasca *devoto*.

He held the glass jar up and examined the color. It seemed just right. The smoky humus smell filled his nostrils. He took a breath of air and then took a sip, letting the bitter fluid burn its way down to his stomach. Then he drained the entire jar.

Sometimes nausea would come right away, but not tonight. There was that initial tiny jolt deep inside his brain— what the old brujo who had taught him the recipe so many years ago had called *el espíritu traqueteando la puerta*, the spirit rattling the door. Dan made his way over to the couch and sat down. He moved a small trash can nearer to him in case nausea came later. He made himself comfortable, breathed slowly, and waited.

The trick to mastering the oracular powers of ayahuasca, Dan had found over the years, was to invite that spirit in as a friend, to collaborate with it, to ask it for help, but to submit to its methods.

And tonight he needed to ask it for a special favor. He had to talk with Magali again. He focused on her, on his memory of her, her hair, her face, her body, her smell, her essence... Memories of nights of lovemaking flooded over him, the way she would kiss him; the way she would work her way under him, moving him on top of her; the way she would open up, letting him feel the dampness between her legs; the way she wrapped those legs around him, pulling him deeper inside of her, rocking with him so that he could thrust into her harder and harder...

He closed his eyes. A deep sadness overtook him. He missed her so much. He could hear a distant roar, like a far-away ocean, that seemed to come from inside his head. Then he heard her voice.

"You called?" she asked.

Dan opened his eyes. Magali was standing... or rather, floating... a few feet away. He blinked his eyes several times to try and see her better. She slowly came into focus until she appeared almost solid. He looked at her. She was almost human, almost flesh-like.

"Did you decide to become a ghost?" he asked.

She shrugged and said, "No, but I needed to stay here for a little while."

"You shouldn't stay a ghost, Magali," Dan said sadly. "You'll be trapped here forever."

"I know," she said, and walked over and sat down on the couch next to him. "You told me that in the cemetery."

Having her sit so close caused a wave of emotions to

wash over Dan. She looked so real. Her lips looked soft. Her eyes glistened with light. Her hair seemed to be moving as if in a soft slow-motion breeze. He thought he could almost smell perfume. His hand rose up and started to move a few inches towards her, but he stopped it in mid-air. He wanted to touch her so much, but knew he could not. He tried to focus on his agenda. He had asked ayahuasca to summon Magali for a purpose.

"Magali," he said, "you can't go back to Antonia. You're killing her. She's wasting away. You have to stop going into her dreams. We're not designed to make love with ghosts. Our bodies can't take it. You have to let her live."

Magali nodded her head slowly, then said, "She was the only one who really loved me."

"I loved you too, Magali," Dan blurted out without thinking.

"You loved the sex, Dan. Men love the sex. Antonia was the only one who never wanted to use me."

Dan shook his head. He could never argue with her when she was alive, and he couldn't argue with her now. It was true: If he had really loved her, he would not have left her. And when images of her arose in his mind, it was always about the sex... the intense sex.

"But," Magali said, "you can tell Antonia I won't enter her dreams anymore. I don't seem to have enough energy to go back. I think my search is over and I have to leave soon."

Ayahuasca was coursing through Dan's body now. There was a loud roaring in his ears.

"And... and what were you searching for, Magali?" he asked.

"The man who took my life. I wasn't supposed to die so young, so I had to stay until I found him."

"And you found him?" Dan asked.

"Yes, I found him."

"Where?" Dan asked.

"Down by the Perequete River... in a garage. He and

the other man were there."

"I promise you, Magali, we will get them!" Dan exclaimed. "We will arrest them and put them in jail for the rest of their lives!"

Magali smiled, "Oh, I don't care about that. You can let them go. I just wanted to see who it was, but I don't care what happens to him."

"Magali, he killed you!"

Magali looked at Dan in the softest, kindest way, and said, "It doesn't matter, Dan. When you're alive, you don't understand because everything seems so real... but life... life is just a dream... and in dreams, nothing really matters..."

Her body began to glow, to become translucent. She looked around the room. "I wonder if I'll miss this," she said out loud. Then she shook her head and added softly, "No, probably not. It's all so.... so thin."

"Magali," Dan said, "Don't go—I've got so many questions..."

"I'm being pulled away, Dan... There is only so much energy that is allotted to us... and when it's gone... it's gone... I wish I had understood that before."

"Magali, *why* did they kill you?"

Magali frowned. "Why?" she said. She appeared to be thinking, then she turned and looked away as if she was looking at something very far away. "I don't know," she finally said. "I don't think he had a reason."

Her body began to pulsate, to glow and fade at the same time.

"Magali," Dan cried, "No... please... no..."

She smiled and shook her head no. "I'm being pulled away, Dan... It's like you told me in the cemetery. I'm dead. I no longer exist."

She became totally transparent, just a glowing pulsating light.

And then, she was gone.

Dan grabbed at the air, pulling it apart, trying to create an opening to the other side, as if he could follow her. For the briefest moment, he thought he saw a swirling river of spirits circling in an infinite spiral, being pulled downward into a black hole. But he couldn't look—it was too vast, too infinite. He felt the breath go out of him. He squeezed his eyes shut. When he opened them again, there was just the empty space on the couch where she had been sitting.

And then the nausea hit him hard. He grabbed the trash can and began to puke.

Chapter Twenty-Six

The next day, some three hundred forty miles away, in the city of Medellín, Colombia, a meeting was being held in the tenth floor executive suite of the Hotel D'Arlez. Three beefy men were sitting in the living room, smoking cigars, and drinking aguardiente over ice. A young woman in a negligee was in the kitchenette refilling the ice bucket when there was a knock on the door. She put down the ice bucket and went to the door and looked through the peephole.

"The other two girls are here, don Mateo," she called out to one of the fat men.

"Put them in the back bedroom, Sugar," the man replied, "and stay with them until we get there. We have some business to discuss for a few more minutes.

The woman opened the door, let in the two other women, and gestured for them to follow her to the bedroom. All three of these women were stunning Colombian beauties, and they were there to have sex with the three men. These men considered it their genteel custom to gather together each week to discuss business, and then to have a bit of entertainment. The duty of arranging the entertainment rotated to a different man each week. This week the duty had fallen to don Mateo, the leader of the group. The other two men watched the three women walk into the bedroom, and nodded their approval to don Mateo.

When the bedroom door was closed, don Mateo spoke.

"As I was saying, gentlemen, we lost another shipment in Panama this week," he said gravely. "That's the fourth one this year. Same scenario: Shipping the truck from Cartagena to Colón goes fine, but the truck disappears once it gets past Panama City. However, we have a lead. On this last truck we installed a newer GPS tracker, and we discovered that the truck detoured around the condos and continued about sixteen kilometers southwest *past* La Chorrera. Then the device stopped transmitting. So somewhere between Colón and La Chorrera is where the truck is getting hijacked. But they have to take it somewhere where they can completely dismantle the truck—otherwise they would not have been able to find the tracker. But we have a pretty good fix on its last location, so I decided to send El Buitre there to resolve this problem.

"El Buitre?" one of the men said. "He'll leave a mess."

"Yes," the third man said, "We don't want him spoiling our investments there."

"We'll have no investments left if this hijacking continues," said don Mateo. "I know he's messy, but we have no choice. These hijackers must be stopped. If they continue there will be nothing left for us. I did have a little talk with him and explained that we didn't want to draw any attention from the federales."

"Yeah," the third man sneered. "I had that same talk with him last year about getting rid of Sanchez in Bogotá, and you know how *that* went... but I have to agree with you, we probably have no other option. He's crude but effective."

The second man nodded his agreement, then asked don Mateo, "When does he leave?"

"He's already left," said don Mateo.

Chapter Twenty-Seven

"Dani, Dani, wake up!"

Don Fernando had dragged Dan's comatose body over to the bed and had hoisted him up onto the mattress. Now he was patting Dan's face with a wet washcloth.

"Come on Dani, wake up."

Dan groaned, opened one eye, looked at don Fernando, closed his eye and winced, and said, "Aw shit fuck, don Fernando."

Don Fernando smiled. He had seen Dan in worse shape.

Dan opened both eyes, squinted and looked around the room. He was relieved to see he was in his own bedroom.

"How long was I out?" he asked don Fernando.

"Just a day," don Fernando said. "I didn't hear from you all day yesterday so I came over this morning."

Dan frowned and asked, "What day is it?"

"Wednesday."

"Shit fuck," Dan said again, then asked, "Is there any coffee?"

"I'll make some," don Fernando said. "You might want to shower and change your clothes."

Dan looked down at his clothes. There were vomit stains all over his shirt and his pants were stained at the crotch where he had pissed himself.

"Shit fuck," he said again and forced himself to get up. He moved slowly and got a pair of clean underwear from the drawer and a clean shirt and pants from the closet and then made his way into the bathroom. Don Fernando went into the kitchen to make coffee.

When the coffee was ready, don Fernando poured two cups and took them out to the small table on Dan's balcony. He went back to the kitchen and found some bread in the refrigerator and placed several pieces on a plate and took that out to the balcony. Then, he sat down in one of the two plastic chairs by the table, and waited for Dan to finish showering.

Dan came out to the balcony a few minutes later, wearing fresh clothes. He grabbed his coffee cup as he sat down and took a sip.

"Thanks," he said to don Fernando. "I need this."

He reached over and eagerly took a piece of the bread on the plate and ate it. Don Fernando waited patiently for Dan to speak.

After eating several more pieces of bread, and drinking half his cup of coffee, Dan spoke. "I talked with Magali last night... no wait, it must have been Monday night, the night before last night... anyway, she said she found the man who killed her, that he is somewhere down by the Perequete River in a garage..."

"That would be Lucas Antigua Martin," don Fernando said and frowned. "My men went down to arrest him at his truck repair shop by the Perequete River yesterday morning, but he wasn't there. There was a truck there—completely dismantled—but no Lucas. He's completely disappeared. We're still searching for him.

Dan thought about this for a moment. He knew the ayahuasca was out of his system, yet he had the strangest feeling of being able to see the image of Lucas Antigua Martin's fat body sprawled out on the ground.

"I wonder if he's dead," Dan said.

Don Fernando looked at Dan's face, trying to see if Dan was just speculating.

"Why do you think that, Dani?" he asked.

"Just a feeling, that's all," Dan said. "And the other man with Lucas? What about him?"

"What other man?" Don Fernando asked.

"Magali said there was another man in the garage with this Lucas guy on Monday... that the other man was some kind of partner with him in this counterfeiting—or whatever it is they were doing..."

"Ahh... Hernán," don Fernando said.

"Probably," Dan answered. "Any leads on him?"

"No," don Fernando said, "Nothing so far. I've got a man at the Tocumen Airport going through all the ticket reservations, both incoming and outgoing... but, so far, nothing. Jenny gave a description of the man, but it could fit many colombianos—she only saw him for a moment... but I have distributed that description to other police forces, especially the border police."

Dan started thinking out loud. "I wonder if they've already left the country, or if they're getting ready to leave... Maybe they got what they wanted... whatever that is... and if that's true, they'd have no reason to stay... they've eliminated their witnesses..."

Don Fernando thought about this for a moment, then reached into his pocket and got his cell phone. He dialed Jorge Manuel's number.

"Hola Koke, it's Fernando... yes, well, thank you. Listen, do me a favor. You remember that fellow in that bar that you and I visited about a week ago? Yes, Rodriguez, the brother of the bar owner, yes. Well, um... go and arrest him, would you... Charge? Oh, I don't know, make one up. I'll come over to your jail this afternoon. I want to have another chat with him. Okay. Thanks, Koke."

Don Fernando put his phone back in his pocket. "I should have leaned on him more last week, found out more about this Hernán guy," he said to Dan. "This Rodriguez fellow told me that he had visited Hernán in Villa Rosario, but he claimed Hernán was just a friend, that he wasn't involved in drugs. I could kick myself for not taking him to the jail then and finding out more."

Dan nodded. "Well, we didn't know then what we know now."

"Yes, that's true."

"But we still don't know much, don Fernando," Dan said. "I still don't see how all the pieces fit together."

Don Fernando nodded in agreement, then asked, "What about that other girl who worked for Jenny, the skinny one we visited… Antonia?"

Dan stared off into the distance. "Well, I think only Lucas knew her. I don't have a feeling that this Hernán guy knew who she was… but you still have someone watching her place, right?"

"Yes."

"Well, it's probably best to keep him there for a while."

Don Fernando nodded in agreement.

"Okay, Dani. Do you want to come with me this afternoon to La Chorrera to chat with this Rodriguez fellow?"

"No, thank you, don Fernando. I think I will just stay around here today and rest."

"Okay, well, I will leave you to recuperate," don Fernando said and stood up to leave.

Chapter Twenty-Eight

After leaving Dan's apartment, don Fernando ran a few errands, then drove back to his office. However, before he could leave for La Chorrera, he received a frantic call from Jorge Manuel.

"Uncle! We went to the Ébano Bar to arrest that fellow Rodriguez this morning, but he is dead! Both him and his brother!"

"Calm down, Koke," don Fernando said. "Take a breath and tell me exactly what happened."

"We went there right after you called me. I took two other officers, in case there were any problems arresting him. But when we got there, we saw that there were three or four of their customers just standing around outside talking. They said that the bar was open but that there was no one inside. So we went in to investigate, and we found both Rodriguez and his brother in one of the back rooms. They had been tied up and shot in the head. Both are dead. My men are working the crime scene now, but I wanted to call you right away."

"I see, I see..." don Fernando said. He knew his nephew didn't have much experience, but he decided to ask anyway. "Tell me, Koke, any idea how long they had been dead?"

"The bodies were cold, uncle. There was a lot of blood, but the edges of the blood were all dry, but only the middle part was wet, so I think they were killed last night, probably after the bar closed. We interviewed the people standing around—some of them had been there when the bar closed, and said everything was normal."

"Ah, good work, Koke," don Fernando said, impressed

that his nephew had been so observant. "Let me know what else your investigation turns up."

"Okay, uncle."

His nephew still sounded upset, so don Fernando added, "Relax, Koke, it's just another murder. Treat it like you would any other crime scene. Call me later."

Okay, uncle. Thank you." And Jorge Manuel hung up. He sat there at his desk, just thinking, drumming his fingers rapidly on the desktop. He tried to put himself in Lucas' place... Why kill the prostitutes? To get his money back? Then why kill Rodriguez? Maybe like Dani had said that morning, to eliminate witnesses...

Don Fernando picked up his phone and buzzed the front desk sergeant.

"Gabriel, who is guarding that Antonia girl?"

"Um, right now, we have Gerardo, Capitán."

"Okay, put another man with him. I want two men guarding her around the clock."

"Sí, Capitán."

"And round up two more good officers and a patrol car and have them meet me by my car in five minutes.'

"Sí, Capitán."

Don Fernando could not shake the bad feeling he had in his chest as he drove over to the La Pitalita neighborhood. Now there were four dead people, all associated with either Lucas or Hernán, and two of them were innocent women. And now the killings were getting more violent. Clearly, Lucas... or Hernán... or both... wanted to eliminate every witness, just like Dani had said.

He turned on his car's siren and flashing lights to get around traffic. Behind him followed the second patrol car with two officers. But when don Fernando pulled into the section of La Pitalita where Rosa lived, he turned off the siren and lights. He was hoping he was wrong.

Rosa was not in the front yard this time. No laundry hung on the line. Don Fernando parked in front and signaled for his two men to follow him as he pushed open the fence gate and walked quickly up to the front door.

"Upe! Upe!" he called out, "Doña Rosa, are you home?"

The front door was open. There was no screen door. He reached in and knocked loudly on the opened door, and yelled out, "Doña Rosa!"

There was no answer. He turned around and gestured to his two men to each go around the opposite sides of the house. Then he stepped inside, and as he did so, he reached to his hip, undid the safety strap on his gun, and rested his hand on the handle.

"Upe! Upe! Doña Rosa," he said and stepped into the living room.

Everything seemed to be in disarray. The floor was littered with items as if they had thrown there. A desk in the corner had all the drawers pulled out, and their contents had been dumped on the floor. Don Fernando removed his gun from his holster, and peered into the kitchen. It was even more of a mess. Every single cabinet drawer was open. Pots and pans had been dumped into heaps on the floor.

He stepped down a short hallway and carefully peered around the door frame into the bedroom. On the other side of the bed he could see a pair of twisted legs sticking out. He glanced quickly around the room and then stepped over to the bed.

Rosa was lying facedown on the floor, her arms tied behind her back. Blood matted the hair on the back of her head and covered the floor around her head. Don Fernando could tell from the color of the blood that she had bled out many hours ago. He slipped his gun back into his holster, and bent down to touch her skin. It was cold.

As he stood up, one of his two men ran into the room.

"Capitán, there is a body in the backyard!" the policeman shouted. Then he saw Rosa's feet sticking out from behind the bed, and instinctively made the sign of the cross on his head and chest.

Don Fernando grunted, "Show me."

The officer led don Fernando to a ditch in the backyard where the other officer was standing. There, sprawled out in the dirt, was the shirtless body of Lucas Antigua Martin. He too had been shot in the head, but don Fernando was staring more at the burn marks all over his arms and chest.

"Don't touch anything," don Fernando said. "Call Vicente. Have him bring his forensic kit and as many men as he needs. Tell him to work the whole house and the yard. Put guards on this house until he is finished. I want to catch whoever did this. I'm going over to Señor Landes' apartment but I'll be available by cell phone."

"Sí, Capitán," said both of the men in unison.

When don Fernando got to Dan's apartment, Dan was still sitting on his balcony. He had made a second pot of coffee and was just gazing out at the vista over the central valley and thinking about Magali. He heard don Fernando's heavy steps coming up the stairway on the side of the building and turned to look. As soon as he saw don Fernando's face, he knew there had been trouble.

"We have problems, Dani," don Fernando said.

"I can tell. What's wrong?" Dan replied.

"Rosa and Lucas are dead!"

"Who's Rosa?" Dan asked.

"Magali's mother. She lives in La Pitalita, and I think that Hernán was staying with her. I got a call from Jorge Manuel this morning—they found Rodriguez dead in his brother's bar in La Chorrera..."

"Wait, don Fernando, Rodriguez is the guy we were talking about this morning, right? He's the one who told Luna that Magali was using drugs." Dan asked.

"Right," don Fernando replied. "He told Luna, and Luna told Jenny, and Jenny told me. Rodriguez was a pimp who managed a couple of whores in the back of his brother's bar in La Chorrera. So, like I said this morning, I went over to the bar last week and leaned on him a bit, and he admitted that he was friends with a colombiano named Hernán who lived here in Villa Rosario. That's why I asked Koke to arrest him this morning"

"And Koke is Jorge Manuel?" Dan asked.

"Right, it's a family name," don Fernando explained.

"Jesus fuck Christ! I can't keep track... okay, run through what happened today again," Dan said.

"So I called Koke and asked him to arrest Rodriguez," don Fernando said.

"Right."

"But when Koke gets to the bar, both Rodriguez and his brother are dead."

"Burundanga?" Dan asked.

"No, they were killed the old fashioned way, Dani—a bullet to the back of the head. Both victims had their hands tied behind their back."

"Shit."

"Yes, and then I got worried, so I drove over to Rosa's house, and both she and Lucas Antigua Martin had been shot the same way, except that Lucas had been tortured before he was shot."

"What? How?" Dan asked.

"Some kind of hot branding iron. My men are processing the house now."

Dan felt overwhelmed. Suddenly he looked up and said, "Antonia... Is she..."

But don Fernando interrupted him. "I've already put an extra guard on her."

Dan leaned back in his chair, closed his eyes, and took a deep breath. He tried to turn his cop brain on, but it just wasn't working today. He felt lost.

"Let's think this through, don Fernando," he said out loud. "Let's just walk through it... Lucas gives Magali and Luna money. Then he wants it back, so he kills both of them to get it... He and Hernán are working together, but it's Lucas who's using burundanga... but where does he learn that technique? From Hernán? Because he's from Colombia?

Or maybe Lucas isn't the killer... maybe it's Hernán, and he has to go after the girls because Lucas is so stupid that he pays them in the counterfeit money they're printing... but suddenly some pimp who knows Hernán is shot... and then someone shoots Lucas... fuck shit... it makes no sense... Okay, let's assume Hernán is the source of the burundanga because he's from Colombia. And he either is the killer of the two girls or he teaches Lucas how to use it... Then why would he kill Rodriguez with a gun? Why would he kill Magali's mom with a gun? Why torture Lucas? Because he's mad at him? No, it's because he wants information out of him. But then why use a gun to kill him? Guns are loud..."

Suddenly Dan opened his eyes. "There's another killer involved, don Fernando!" he almost shouted. "That's why a gun's involved! Someone else has come here!"

Dan knew the ayahuasca was long out of his system, but he also knew the feeling he got when ayahuasca started connecting the dots for him.

"Don't you see, don Fernando?" Dan said. "Someone new has come to town—someone who wants to find Hernán—that means someone from Colombia is here. Why Colombia? Because Hernán is a renegade from some cartel. So they've sent an enforcer, and he kills Rodriguez to find out where Hernán is. And he kills Rodriguez's brother simply because he's a witness. Rodriguez tells him that Hernán is living with Magali's mother, so this guy comes to Villa Rosario and goes to her house... but Hernán is not there... but Lucas happens to be there for some reason... wrong place wrong time... and this guy kills Magali's mother and then tortures Lucas until Lucas tells him where Hernán is... and then this guy kills Lucas and goes to find Hernán."

"And who is this new killer, and where is Hernán?" don Fernando asked.

Dan closed his eyes and tried to summon ayahuasca. He took a deep breath and tried to empty his mind.

Then he opened his eyes and said quietly, "He's a thug... big... merciless... and he's already found Hernán."

Chapter Twenty-Nine

Deep in the jungle, miles from Villa Rosario, a fat man was tending a small fire in a small clearing. Despite the shade provided by the jungle canopy, the air was hot and humid, and the fat man was sweating profusely. He was sitting on a small stump of wood, carefully turning a metal poker in the fire. He used a thick piece of cloth to hold the poker, and would occasionally pull it out of the fire to check the color of the glowing metal point. Next to the fire, a dark thin man was tied naked to a tree. His head was bruised and bloody and hung to one side. His arms were stretched backwards around the tree, and tied at the wrists. Duct tape covered his mouth. His naked legs were pulled wide apart and staked to the ground at the ankles with rope and crudely fashioned wooden stakes.

The fat man shifted his weight on the wooden stump so that he faced the tied-up man. Then he reached back and retrieved the metal poker from the fire. The tip was white hot. He gently touched the glowing tip to the man's chest. A muffled scream came from under the duct tape as the tied-up man's body jerked away from the poker. The tied-up man stared up at the fat man, eyes wide in total fear.

"Ah good. You're awake," the fat man said. "I'm only going to explain this once, so listen carefully."

The fat man held the glowing tip up and blew on it. Tiny sparks flew off. He placed it back in the fire and then reached into his pocket and pulled out a small 9-millimeter pistol and held it up for the tied-up man to see.

"I'm going to kill you. There is no way out. First, you

are going to tell me where the money is, and then I'm going to kill you. If you tell me right now, I'll just shoot you quickly and you will die quickly. But if you do not tell me right now, I will burn every part of your body, starting with your pecker... Here, let me show you..."

The fat man took the cloth and grabbed the poker out of the fire, raised it over the man's spread legs and jabbed it hard into the man's scrotum. The flesh seared and stank as the tied-up man's body convulsed against the ropes that held him. He started hyperventilating through his nose. Tears poured out of his eyes.

"Yes, that's pain," the fat man said, and placed the poker back into the fire. "As I was saying, you tell me what I want to know, and I will kill you quickly. You don't tell me, or if I think you're lying to me, I will burn off your pecker, and then I will burn out your eyes, and I will continue burning you until you are dead. And it makes no difference to me. My assignment is only to find you and kill you. But, if you tell me where the money is, I will shoot you in the head and you will die quickly. It's your choice."

The fat man paused and stared down at the tied-up man. Then he reached back into a small satchel that sat behind the wooden stump and pulled out a long thin knife. He leaned over his victim, grabbed the man's head with his large left hand to hold it steady, and cut off one of the man's ears. The man screamed behind the duct tape as blood gushed down the side of his head.

The fat man threw the ear into the fire and watched it sizzle and turn black in the flames. Then he turned to the man again.

"That was in case you didn't believe me," the fat man said. "Now, I'm going to remove the duct tape and I'm only going to ask you one time. If you bullshit me, you will suffer so much agony that you will beg me to kill you. If you tell me straight, you will die quickly."

The fat man reached down, grabbed a corner of the

duct tape and ripped it half off the man's face so that it hang from the other side of the man's head.

"You have ten seconds to tell me," the fat man said.

Chapter Thirty

Don Fernando called Dan every day for the next week to update him on the murders. Each day brought forth a new piece of information, but nothing that seemed to connect the dots for Dan. Each of the four shooting victims who had been shot by the same gun—but that news did not surprise Dan. Rosa had the same tattoo on her shoulder of a clock without hands that Luna had. Lucas also had the same tattoo on his shoulder, as did Rodriguez. That news was interesting, but did not particularly surprise Dan, either. Rodriguez's brother did not have a tattoo—but that made sense; he was probably not involved in the case. Don Fernando's men at the Tocumen Airport could not find anyone named Hernán flying into or out of Panama City who fit the description that Jenny had provided—but that also did not surprise Dan. He couldn't erase the image in his head of some big enforcer from Colombia holding Hernán captive. Dan simply assumed Hernán was dead. On the fifth day, however, don Fernando called Dan at home with news that did surprise him.

"Dani," don Fernando said, "I just got off the phone with Dr. María José Vargas at the Forensic Laboratory in Panama City."

"Yeah?"

"She says those twenty dollar bills are not counterfeit."

"What?" Dan exclaimed.

"She said they are authentic," don Fernando said.

"Fuck, don Fernando!" Dan said, "Is she sure?"

"That's what she told me, Dani, but she sent them to the FBI laboratory some place in Quan... Quanico?" don Fernando said.

"Quantico?" Dan said, "In Virginia? Why?"

"Yes, there. I don't know why," don Fernando said. "She just said that the money was not counterfeit, but she sent the bills to Quantico to be sure."

"Shit... okay, don Fernando, I need to think about this. Let me call you later."

"Okay, Dani."

After don Fernando hung up, Dan poured a cup of cold coffee from the morning's coffee pot, heated it up in the microwave, and took it out to his balcony chair to sit and think. This changed everything. Now nothing about the case made sense. If Lucas wasn't trying to get counterfeit money back from Magali and Luna, then what the fuck was he searching for? What was so important that he had to kill them? Anger rose in Dan's throat. Magali's death was now totally senseless, a total waste of someone he loved. Then he remembered something she had said during her last visit—that maybe the man who killed her didn't have a reason. Dan felt tears behind his eyes, and he tried to push them back. He forced his cop brain to turn on. He had to think. He knew that when a case turned cold, it was always important to go back to the very beginning and reconstruct it again. So he sat there on his balcony, going over every fact from the beginning, trying to remember everything Magali had said to him, every vision ayahuasca had given him, and trying on every hypothesis he could think of. When he finished his cup of coffee, he went back inside to the kitchen and brewed a new pot. When did life become so fucked up? he wondered. He had just wanted to retire to Panama and live a quiet life. Why couldn't he have loved Magali when he had the chance? He pushed those feelings back down and went over the facts again. Lucas came into some money. That money was new twenty dollar bills, but they weren't counterfeit. Lucas spent the money on prostitutes, but then for some reason had to get the money back. Luna knew Rodriguez, and they both had a tattoo of a faceless clock on their shoulders, as did Magali's mother, but not

Magali. Magali did not know Luna. Drugs didn't seem to be involved, except someone, probably Lucas—but maybe Hernán—planted drugs on Magali to make her death look like a drug overdose. But he didn't do that with Luna. Was he getting sloppy because he was desperate? And then a third man shows up. All Dan knew about this guy was that he was big and vicious. Magali hadn't mentioned him, so he had come onto the scene after she died. Maybe that was why Lucas had become more frantic about getting his money back. But where did the money come from? Hernán had to have been the catalyst for the money. Lucas didn't have a pot to piss in before Hernán showed up. But where did Lucas get the money? Maybe it *was* drugs, because there was that dismantled truck in Lucas' garage. Maybe they were stealing drug shipments from some Colombian cartel—a cartel that Hernán used to belong to—and that was why the cartel sent an enforcer to stop them... But if they were stealing drugs, and selling them for cash, why were there no spikes in drug arrests or other indications of a sudden influx of drugs? Maybe they weren't distributing them in Panama. Were they just diverting the drugs and putting them on another truck out of Panama? And then getting paid by some other cartel, maybe a Mexican cartel? Somebody had to be giving Hernán money for something... and he was paying Lucas to use his garage. Had Lucas introduced him to Rosa? How involved had Rosa been?

Dan sat on his balcony for over two hours, going over and over the facts. But nothing made any sense. His head hurt. He felt horribly frustrated and angry. And old. Maybe he had lost his touch.

It was late afternoon when he left his balcony and went inside to his computer and emailed don Fernando a list of questions to send to Jorge Manuel and to Dr. Vargas. After he sent that email, he went over to the cabinet and took out the whiskey bottle.

Chapter Thirty-One

The next day, Dan asked don Fernando to drive him over to visit Antonia. The two guards on Antonia's apartment were under strict orders not to let anyone in except Jenny, so Dan needed don Fernando to be there to get past the guards. Dan wasn't sure why he wanted to see her—in part it was to assure himself that she was getting better; in part it was to ask her some more question; but mostly it was simply to see and appreciate the person whom Magali said was the only one who truly loved her.

When they arrived, don Fernando chatted briefly with the two officers, and commended them on their vigilance. Then he and Dan made their way through the narrow alley up to Antonia's apartment. She answered when Dan knocked at her door.

Dan was glad to see that she looked much better. She no longer looked anorexic. Her skin had a good color, her eyes were bright, and she smiled when she saw them.

She invited them inside and they sat in the same seats that they had sat in eight days earlier.

"You look so much better, Antonia," Dan said.

She smiled and said, "Yes, thank you. I can sleep at night now."

"Magali no longer comes to you in your dreams," Dan stated.

Antonia smiled but shook her head sadly, "No, not since you two were here. I have not seen her since."

"You won't see her again," Dan said. "I mean, you might dream about her, but it would just be a dream. She is no longer here to enter your body and take over your dreams. She's gone now."

"Where did she go, Señor Landes?" Antonia asked.

"She went into the earth. She told me that's where all spirits go after they die, if they don't want to be ghosts and stay here forever, and she didn't want to do that."

Don Fernando sat quietly. He decided he was going to keep his mouth shut on this visit.

"Yes, that makes sense, Señor Landes. She was always talking about being pulled down to the center of the world. She kept saying that she wanted to stay here just a little longer, but she knew she would have to leave soon."

"Can I tell you something nice she said about you?" Dan asked.

"Yes, please," Antonia said and smiled.

"She said you were the only person who ever loved her—who never wanted anything from her, never wanted to use her," Dan said.

Antonia nodded her head and looked down. When she raised her face back up to Dan, her eyes were moist and shining. "Yes, she was a special woman... I always thought she had an old soul, you know, a soul who had been born and died millions of times."

Dan thought about this for a moment.

"You know, Antonia, when she came to see me, she kept saying that dying didn't matter... or rather... that now that she was dead, that nothing in life seemed to matter... She didn't seem to care whether we caught the man who killed her, for example. One of the last things she said to me was that she wasn't going to miss life, that it was too 'thin', she had said. I wanted to tell her that wasn't true. I think being alive does matter. I think right and wrong matter..."

"Maybe it's just different when you're dead," Antonia offered. "Maybe both worlds are true, but each have their own pushes and pulls. She was being pulled to the center of the world... maybe we are pulled upward..."

Dan nodded. The thought crossed his mind that maybe Antonia was an old soul, too.

"Yes," he said. I told her she couldn't enter your dreams

anymore because human beings are not designed to be in love with ghosts. It... It deteriorates us, eats away at us... Our bodies can't take it."

Antonia got a faraway look in her eye. "It's odd, isn't it? How we yearn for something that eats away at us..."

Dan wasn't sure if she was referring to love or to death, but he just nodded.

"Antonia, I have to ask you if Magali ever said anything to you in your dreams that might be a clue as to why she died or who these people were?"

"No, señor. She just said none of it was important."

Dan shook his head. "I think it's important, Antonia."

Antonia nodded. "I do too, Señor Landes. I hope you catch them."

"Thank you Antonia," Dan said. "We're going to go now. Thank you for letting us visit."

"You're welcome. By the way, how much longer will those policemen stay here? I would like to go back to work soon."

Dan looked over at don Fernando, but don Fernando gave no response, so Dan said, "Just a little while longer, Antonia. Give us a couple more days. We just want to be extra sure."

Antonia nodded. The two men stood up and left.

Outside in the alleyway, don Fernando muttered quietly to Dan, "That was the most bizarre visit I've ever had to sit through, Dani."

Chapter Thirty-Two

Two days after don Fernando's phone call about the money being real, don Fernando called Dan again with some more surprising news.

"Dani, the FBI is coming to meet with us."

"What? What for?"

"I'm not sure. Dr. Vargas called me this morning. She said that she got a phone call today from Quanico…"

"Quantico."

"Yes, from the FBI laboratory there, and they are sending some agent down who wants to meet with all of us," don Fernando explained.

"Really?"

"Yes, he will be here tomorrow afternoon, Dani. Dr. Vargas is going to meet him at the airport and drive him to La Chorrera…"

Don Fernando paused, and then said, "Can I pick you up tomorrow afternoon and we'll go to La Chorrera?"

"Oh fuck, don Fernando," Dan said.

"Please Dani. I don't know if this agent can speak Spanish or not, and someone needs to tell him everything about this case," don Fernando said.

"Why do we have to tell him everything about the case?" Dan asked.

"Because that's why he's coming down here, Dani. The FBI told Dr. Vargas that this agent needs to know everything we know about the case and then he will explain why."

"Uh huh," Dan said, "So we have to first tell him everything we know, and then—maybe—he'll tell us why he wants to know? Shit, don Fernando, that's so typical of the FBI. They think they're so goddamn important."

"But Dani, what do we have to lose? We are stuck,

and have no leads... well, we have one new one. Jorge Manuel found the tattoo artist who did the clock tattoos."

"Really?" Dan said.

"Yes, he is questioning him today. He will tell us tomorrow at the meeting what he found out."

"The meeting?" Dan asked.

"The meeting with the FBI agent. Please come, Dani..." don Fernando said, then added coyly, "María José Vargas will be there."

That made Dan smile. "Okay, don Fernando, but only for that reason."

"Thank you Dani," don Fernando said. "I told Jorge Manuel that you would lead the discussion and explain the case to the FBI agent."

"Oh? So you knew I would come?" Dan said in mock outrage.

"Well, when I heard that Dr. Vargas was going to be there, Dani, I naturally assumed you would want to help," don Fernando said. "Can I pick you up at one tomorrow?"

"Yeah, okay, amigo. See you then," Dan replied and hung up.

Dan sat there and thought a bit. He had worked with FBI agents in his past life as a detective, and he never really cared for them. They always looked and acted the same: young, clean-cut, white, emotionless robots. But don Fernando was right—they had nothing to lose by talking to this agent, because they were stuck in the case. He didn't mind summarizing the case for the agent, but he was going to have to figure out how he could explain certain things without saying he had talked with Magali's ghost.

Chapter Thirty-Three

The next day, don Fernando drove Dan to the police station in La Chorrera. Dan had managed to find a tie to wear, and had ironed a shirt. Don Fernando also brought Vicente Castaneda, his forensic officer, with him. Jorge Manuel welcomed them into the large conference room. There were six chairs arranged around the conference table with six packets of documents and photographs at each position. The men all sat and waited for Dr. Vargas and the FBI agent to show up. As usual in Panama, airplane arrivals were always late, but Jorge Manuel had arranged coffee on a small side table with small bocadillos to snack on while they waited. Thirty minutes later, Dr. Vargas arrived with the FBI agent.

The agent turned out not to be so young, and certainly not white. He was an older African-American man, with graying hair, impeccably dressed in a dark suit. It had been Dan's experience that all FBI agents always wore the same type of dark suit. Dan assumed it was agency-issued.

Dan would have preferred to have made some small talk with the agent before the meeting started, but the circumstances did not permit it. Dr. Vargas, as usual, was all business, dressed in a sharp pantsuit, with her hair pulled back in a tight bun. There was something about her serious demeanor that Dan found attractive. It was as if she was wrapped up so tight that she would explode if he could just release one hook. She apologized for being late, nodded hello to Dan, directed the FBI agent to a chair, and motioned for everyone else to sit. And everyone complied. Then don Fernando gave Dan a look that indicated the ball was in his court.

"Well, I guess we can get started with some introductions," Dan said, and nodded hello to the FBI agent. "My name is Dan Landes. I used to be a detective for the Los Angeles police department, but I am retired now and live in the neighboring town of Villa Rosario. I am here in no official capacity, but solely as a friend and guest of don Fernando," and Dan gestured at don Fernando who also nodded to the FBI agent, "who is the police chief of Villa Rosario. And I'm also here as the guest of Jorge Manuel, who is the police chief here in the city of La Chorrera, and whose hospitality we are enjoying here."

Jorge Manuel followed don Fernando's lead and also nodded hello to the FBI agent.

"Also present with us today is Vincent Castaneda, who is the forensic officer in Villa Rosario," Dan continued. "And you've already met Dr. María José Vargas, the head of Toxicology at the Ministry of Justice's Forensic Laboratory in Panama City."

The FBI agent nodded to everyone at the table and introduced himself.

"Thank you all for having me here, especially on such short notice. My name is James Dixon, and I am the Assistant Director of the Southeast Division of the FBI's Financial Fraud Investigation Unit. I understand from Dr. Vargas that your case here involves several murders, and I probably will be of no use to you in resolving that investigation, although I may have a few pieces of information that might fill in the bigger picture. But, to be honest, you may have far more information that helps us, than we have that helps you. But, if you could describe this case to me, from the start, then I can share how that may or may not fit into our work."

At least he is direct, Dan thought to himself, and took a deep breath.

"Fair enough, agent Dixon," Dan said.

"Call me James," the agent said and smiled.

Dan had rarely seen an FBI agent smile. He almost liked this agent. "Okay, fair enough, James. Don Fernando has asked me to take the lead on describing this case. I don't know how much Dr. Vargas has told you, so I will, as you say, start at the beginning. Forgive me if I cover information you already know."

Dan stood up and went over to the blackboard on the wall and wrote:

Rosa -------- Hernán ------ Rodriguez
                    |
Magali ------- Lucas --------- Luna

He went back to his seat, sat down and continued, "It all began a little over three weeks ago when a young prostitute named Magali was found dead..."

Dan paused. "And you should understand, James, that prostitution is treated differently down here than it is in the states. It's legal and it's just a job that some women do. Magali was a well-liked and upstanding member of the community... Anyway, she was found dead in her apartment in Villa Rosario. It appeared to the police that her apartment had been staged to look like she had suffered a drug overdose. There was a line of coke and a syringe full of heroin on her table. But everyone knew that Magali did not use drugs and, in fact, no heroin or cocaine was found in her system. What *was* found in her system was a fatal dose of scopolamine."

Out of the corner of his eye, Dan saw Jorge Manuel frown in confusion, so he added, "Or burundanga, as it's known down here. Burundanga is a drug that occurs naturally in a lot of plants, but in Colombia it is made from a flower called the Devil's Breath. Different methods evolved over the centuries for creating a powder from this plant, and it was used by indigenous tribes in Colombia to induce trances or enslave captives. But recently, Colombian criminals have taken an interest in this drug because it can be mixed in a drink or just discretely blown onto a victim's skin in order to incapacitate them. We know that the drug used to kill Magali was burundanga, and not prescription scopolamine, because Dr. Vargas did the blood toxicology tests and discovered types of impurities in the poison that you would find in homemade burundanga. We believed the killer had to be someone whom Magali knew because you have to be physically very close to a victim in order to administer the powder. Then about two weeks later, another victim turned up, this time a prostitute in La Chorrera. The police started looking for connections between these two girls. The two girls did not know each other, but they did have one thing in common: they both had recently serviced a man named Lucas Antigua Martin. There was a third prostitute, who is currently under police protection, who had also serviced Lucas Antigua Martin, and we know he was trying to find her before he was killed. Lucas was our main suspect in the murders of Magali and Luna, and our hypothesis was that all three prostitutes had something that he wanted. We think that after he killed Magali, he searched her apartment, and it also appeared that he went through Luna's purse after he killed her. We didn't know what he might have been searching for, but then we discovered that he had paid the surviving prostitute in brand new twenty-dollar bills. So we developed a theory—which we now know to be false—that the money was counterfeit, and that Lucas had paid the girls in counterfeit bills but wanted those bills back..."

Dan paused. "I'm getting a bit ahead of myself. Let me back up a bit, because the hypothesis of the counterfeit money was actually our second theory. Our first theory was that this case involved drug trafficking. We had started with that theory, obviously, because of the heroin and cocaine that had been found in Magali's apartment...

"Anyway, this Lucas guy was dirt poor. He didn't have money. He ran a crappy truck repair garage on a rather secluded street on the outskirts of Villa Rosario. But there was a second man involved with Lucas, a man named Hernán. We believe he was Colombian because of his accent and his general appearance. He had come to Villa Rosario only recently, whereas Lucas had lived here all his life.

We don't think Hernán knew any of the three prostitutes, although we do know that he came by the brothel where two of them worked, but the madam of that brothel thought he was creepy and wouldn't let him in. But he was seen with Magali's mother—whose name was Rosa—a few days after Magali's death, and we are pretty sure he was living with her. Her house was near Lucas' garage.

"So our first theory was that somehow Hernán was tied up with drug trafficking. We developed a theory that he was a renegade from some Colombian cartel and that he had enlisted Lucas' aid because Lucas had the garage where they could dismantle cartel trucks they were hijacking. We kept looking for an explanation for why Lucas had so much money all of a sudden. The money had to come from somewhere. But when Jorge Manuel studied the statistics for new drug arrests and other indications of increased drug activity, he found none. We didn't have any evidence that any more drugs were being smuggled through Panama than before Hernán showed up. That's when we started playing with the idea that they were counterfeiting money.

"At that point, we didn't have enough evidence to arrest anyone. So don Fernando decided to question this fellow named Rodriguez," Dan said, pointing to the chalkboard. "Rodriguez was a pimp in a dive bar in La Chorrera, but he knew Luna, and he had also admitted to don Fernando during a prior interview that he knew Hernán, and that Hernán was Colombian, *and* that he had visited Hernán in Villa Rosario. But when Jorge Manuel went to pick him up for questioning, they discovered he had been executed— tied up and shot in the back of the head. Suddenly, we now had a different method of killing, and my belief was that a new suspect had come to town... maybe an enforcer sent by the Colombian cartel. At that point, acting on a hunch, don Fernando went over to Magali's mother's house and found both Rosa and Lucas Antigua Martin tied up and executed in the same way as Rodriguez, the only difference being that Lucas' body had signs of torture, which added to our theory that this Colombian enforcer was looking for Hernán and had tortured Lucas to find out where Hernán was.

"Oh, and I forgot... there is this odd tattoo that keeps showing up—a faceless clock. Luna had it, and her tattoo was recent; Rodriguez had it; Magali's mother had it; and so did Lucas. I think Jorge Manuel found the tattoo artist that maybe did Luna's tattoo, and maybe he has more information on what that's about."

Dan looked up at the chart. "Oh, there's another death. Rodriguez had a brother, who was also executed along with Rodriguez, but we don't think he was involved in any of this.... What else? Well, I guess that's it, except to add that my personal opinion is that Hernán is dead—that whoever killed Rodriguez, his brother, Magali's mother, and Lucas, was too determined and too ruthless to let Hernán escape. Anyway, as you can see, we are left with six dead bodies that we know of, no evidence, no leads, and no... no explanation for why these people died. So any light that the FBI can shed on this case will be helpful. But before I turn the meeting over to you, James, I think we should go around the room and see what other pieces of evidence we have, maybe starting with Jorge Manuel, who I understand interviewed a tattoo artist yesterday about the faceless clock tattoo."

Jorge Manuel looked at don Fernando, and don Fernando nodded to him indicating he should speak.

"We took a photograph of the tattoo on the dead girl's shoulder to all the tattoo parlors in La Chorrera," Jorge Manuel began. "No one claimed to know anything about it, but then we learned that one of the tattoo artists had lied to us, so we went back to visit him. After some, um, coaxing, he told us that he had done the tattoos for the prostitute and for two people from Villa Rosario. He said a thin colombiano brought all three in, but not at the same time. He said that the colombiano brought in a middle aged woman from Villa Rosario first, and about a week later, he brought in a man, also from Villa Rosario. We assume that these were the mother and the man named Lucas," Jorge Manuel said, pointing at Dan's chart on the blackboard. "Then about a week before the prostitute Luna was killed, he had brought her in for a tattoo. The tattoo artist had never met any of these people before, and never saw them again. He said it was just a normal business transaction, except that the colombiano was the one who chose the art and also the one who paid. That part, he said, was unusual—that usually the person receiving the tattoo makes the selection or at least expresses their opinion. But in the case of these three people, the colombiano was in charge, and the clients simply received the tattoo."

"And all three tattoos were placed on the victims' back, on their left shoulder?" Dan asked.

"Sí, señor."

"And how did the colombiano tell the tattoo artist what he wanted? Did he have a diagram or a picture?" Dan asked.

"No, señor. He just took off his shirt. The colombiano had the same tattoo but it was on his chest, over his heart."

"Interesting," Dan said. "Anything else?"

"Yes, the most interesting thing to us was that the colombiano paid in brand new twenty dollar bills."

"Really?" Dan said. "Did he still have any of those bills?"

"Alas no, Señor Landes. He had spent them all."

Jorge Manuel looked like he was finished speaking, so Dan looked over at don Fernando to see if he had anything he wanted to say. But don Fernando simply pointed at his forensic officer Vicente.

"Señor Castaneda," Dan said, addressing Vicente, "do you have any new information for us?"

"Only that we went through the dismantled truck that we found in the garage owned by Lucas Antigua Martin, and examined all the parts that were lying beside the truck as well. This was a typical small transport truck—approximately six meters in length—that is commonly used in most of Central America. We were able to trace the truck to Colombia. According to its manifest, it was carrying high-end plumbing parts—expensive faucets, shower heads, and Jacuzzi tub accessories—that were to be delivered to a condominium project outside of La Chorrera. The truck was loaded in Medellín and was driven straight to Cartagena where it was put on a boat to Colón. When it arrived in Colón, it received a thorough inspection by drug-sniffing dogs. Also, the cargo inside the truck was inspected by customs and it corresponded to the manifest. All the proper documents had been filled out correctly and all the taxes were paid. Nothing appeared out of the ordinary, and the dogs did not detect any drugs. According to our investigation, this truck belonged to a trucking company called Bodegato SA in Colombia that appears to be a legitimate company, and it makes regular deliveries of such products, not only to Panama, but to high-end real estate developments throughout Central and South America.

"All of the cargo of the truck—the plumbing supplies—were stacked in the corner of the garage, still in their original boxes. We opened all the boxes; tested them; tested all the parts of the truck lying on the ground, basically tested the entire truck and all the contents, and found no traces of any drugs. What we did find, however, was that someone, probably Lucas Antigua Martin, had used a cutting torch and diamond-bladed saw to remove the metal plate that was the floor of the truck cabin. Under the metal plate were hollowed-out spaces designed to hold some type of contraband. We don't know what that was, of course. We did test those cavities for any drug residue but found none. That's all we have on the truck."

"Thank you, Vicente," Dan said. "Can you talk a bit about the shooting victims?"

"Yes," Vicente said, thumbing through his notes. "All four victims had their wrists tied behind their backs, and three of the four were shot in the back of the head with a 9-millimeter pistol. All the bullets came from the same gun, and it was fired at point-blank range in each case. We sent photos of the rifling marks to Dr. Vargas' laboratory. The fourth victim, Lucas Antigua Martin, was shot in the side of the head, and his body showed signs of torture, so our assumption was that he lying on his side so that the murderer could torture him and talk to him, and that he was killed after he had provided the information that the murderer wanted."

"And the method of torture?" Dan asked.

"He was burned. The marks were consistent with a metal stick or poker. We think the torture happened inside the house. There was no evidence of a fire outside of the house, but we found scrape marks on the stove's electric burner where the murderer could have heated up the poker. Why the murderer took him outside to kill him, we don't know. Nor do we know if both victims were at the house when the murderer arrived, or whether one or both victims showed up later during the home invasion."

"Home invasion, yes, talk a little bit about that if you can," Dan said.

"Well, clearly someone had torn the house apart, looking for something. We don't think he found it because normally when a burglar finds what they are looking for, they stop searching, so part of the house is not in disarray. But in this case, the entire house was in shambles. We did take fingerprints... actually, the house was filthy and there were about two hundred different prints that we took. We're still working those, but no leads yet. That's really all we have."

"Thank you Vicente," Dan said. Then Dan turned to María José Vargas.

"Dr. Vargas, anything you'd like to add?"

"Just three points, she said. "We do have the photographs of the rifling marks that Corporal Castaneda sent us. We have entered them into our database. Unfortunately, we only started keeping a searchable database of bullet rifling just three years ago. So we don't have a lot of data. We could not find any matches for bullets from that gun in Panama, but that doesn't mean that the gun has not been used for other crimes in Panama. We did send a copy of the rifling marks to the Colombian National Police Forensic Laboratory in Bogotá, but we haven't heard anything back yet.

"Secondly, since Señor Landes brought up the subject of the twenty-dollar bills, I want to explain why we sent them to the FBI laboratory. Our office tested those bills and examined them very carefully under a microscope and under ultraviolet light. As far as we could tell, the bills were authentic. The printing was precise; they had both magnetic and color-changing ink, and the security thread was correct. But there was something that we hadn't seen before—a second security thread on the edge of the bills. We assumed that this was simply a new security feature that we weren't aware of. So I called the United States Treasury in Washington, D.C., to see if they could send us some literature on it, so that we could update our files. But no one there would tell me anything about it—they didn't deny it was a new feature, but they were very hush-hush. I assumed it was for security reasons. I ended up being transferred to Agent Dixon at the FBI, which I thought was rather odd. But after I described our situation and the tests we had done on the bills, he assured me that the bills were authentic, and that this second security thread was indeed a new security feature that was still in the testing mode, and he asked me to send the bills to the FBI laboratory in Quantico so that he could examine them personally, and he said that he would be in touch afterwards. He also asked me to keep this information to myself—because this new security thread was still being tested—and not to share it with anyone until he got back in touch with me. I did not share this information with any of you here before, partly out of professional courtesy to Agent Dixon, but mostly because it seemed irrelevant to this investigation. But this morning, I asked Agent Dixon if I could share it, and he agreed.

"Thirdly, and I think most importantly, I want to talk about the type of burundanga that was in the blood of both of the unfortunate young women. As Señor Landes stated, Scopolamine occurs naturally in many plants: jimson weed, Datura, and plants from the nightshade family. These plants grow in many countries in South America and even here in Panama. But in Colombia, a particularly potent form of Scopolamine occurs in the flower of the Brugmansia tree, sometimes called the borrachero tree. It is the flower of this tree that is known as Devil's Breath. Scopolamine is not a narcotic; rather, it is an alkaloid drug, similar to belladonna and atropine, which depresses the central nervous system. But the poison burundanga from the Devil's Breath flower is an extremely potent version of Scopolamine, and chemically unique, which is why we were able to conclusively say that these two girls were killed with burundanga that originated in Colombia. And thus, we at the Ministry of Justice are very concerned about these recent events."

María José Vargas gestured to Dan that she was finished.

"Thank you, Dr. Vargas," Dan said. He looked around the table to see if anyone had anything more to add, then he turned to Agent Dixon.

"Well, James, that's all we have. Six dead bodies, no motive, and no viable theory about why this all happened. I'll turn the reins over to you now."

Chapter Thirty-Four

James Dixon had been keeping notes during everyone's presentation. When Dan had finished speaking, James put down his pen, folded his hands in front of him, and began to speak.

"Thank you for that overview—that was extremely helpful... really quite excellent detective work... and remarkably close to the truth of what we think is going on. As I mentioned, I am the Assistant Director of the Southeast Division of the FBI's Financial Fraud Investigation Unit. We investigate and prosecute all manner of financial fraud including check fraud, credit card fraud, mortgage fraud, securities fraud, insider trading, tax evasion, embezzlement, identity theft, forgery, money laundering, counterfeiting... the list goes on and on. Depending on the type of crime, we work closely with other state and federal agencies, and with other countries. In fact, there are very few financial crimes that don't involve the jurisdiction of other agencies, states, or countries. The reason we get involved is that many agencies simply don't have the technical resources that the FBI does. Financial frauds are usually very complex, very sophisticated, can span many states or occur on the internet or involve overseas accounts; and this is where the FBI can offer its expertise. Our work is usually behind the scenes— we help gather the evidence that allows other authorities to prosecute cases.

"Usually, cases have to be pretty big for the FBI to take an interest. We really don't like to get involved in a case unless the amount of fraud is at least over a hundred thousand dollars. Money laundering is one of those crimes that usually surpasses that threshold. We are seeing more and more sophisticated money laundering schemes, and more use of shell companies and offshore accounts. To be honest, the Mossack Fonseca scandal was a wake-up call to the amount of money illegally passing through these shell companies."

Dan tried to keep his face expressionless when James made that last comment. He knew that despite the fact that the Panama Papers exposed how the Panamanian law firm Mossack Fonseca had created over 200,000 offshore accounts and shell companies to hide its clients' assets, that only a handful of people were ever prosecuted—mostly small-time tax evaders in the United Kingdom. He also knew the reason why so few gringos were caught up in the scandal—they didn't need Mossack Fonseca to form shell companies in Central America. They could form them faster and easier in Delaware or Wyoming and launder their money inside the US.

James continued speaking. "In fact, our office doubled in size when the Panama Papers were released, just to have the staff to analyze those documents... which brings me to why I'm here.

Dan's ears pricked up.

"It's no secret that Colombia supplies most of the world's cocaine," James said. "Despite a forty-year War on Drugs, the United States has not put a dent in Colombia's ability to transport drugs into the United States and sell them at a huge profit. Now, my department deals with financial fraud—we don't do drug cases. But when the Panama Papers were released, the DEA—the Drug Enforcement Agency—asked us to examine them to see if there was anything in them that could be used as a weapon against the drug cartels. And what we found stunned us.

"Colombia has a total of seventy-six different banks—that's seventy- six different banking corporations, but only twelve of them are Colombian banks. The rest are foreign banks. And in the Panama Papers we found that these banking corporations own more than one thousand shell companies situated throughout the Cayman Islands, the Bahamas, and the Philippines. And these shell companies are often set up as corporations doing business *inside* different foreign banks in those countries. And we have no idea how many other shell companies are owned by these initial shell companies. But the point is, we found a higher number of shell companies connected to Colombian banks than to banks of any other South American country. So, naturally we wondered if they might have been set up to launder money, specifically drug money.

"But... to be perfectly candid with you, that is not a battle that the FBI can win. These offshore accounts and corporations enjoy the protection of those offshore foreign governments, and the FBI cannot pierce that protection. We have no authority over these companies, and to say they are not cooperative with us would be an understatement..."

James paused, then said, "That's not to say we don't pick up information from different sources, or confidential informants....but it does mean that we have to pick the battles we can win." James paused again, took a sip of water, and looked down at his notes, as if he was gathering his thoughts. "One of the items we were focusing on was the immense growth of shell companies connected with land ownership. It appeared to us that, not just one, but all of the Colombian cartels had started to buy land, as a way of laundering money—land in foreign countries. We think the idea originated in the nineties, when the cartels were buying warehouses in California and Arizona simply to have safe places to store their cocaine while it was in transit. But then the real estate market boomed, and the cartels realized, not only how much money they could make when they sold the buildings, but that the process of selling the buildings washed their initial investment clean of any drug connections. So they started buying land in the United States at a furious clip. It was easy because they already had the cash in the US from the drug sales. And during the real estate boom, none of the banks looked at who was buying houses or commercial property. The cartels would use a straw man to buy a house with a subprime mortgage, then the straw man would sell the house to one of the cartel's shell companies in a private sale and pay off the mortgage, and *bingo*—the shell company owned a house or business property, free and clear and completely clean.

"This buying spree in the US came to a halt after the real estate market crashed in 2008, and US banks were suddenly required to look at who was buying property. So the cartels simply started using these shell companies to buy land in other countries... in fact, in many other countries. Their methods depend on the country. In some countries, like the Dominican Republic or the Bahamas, they might build entire all-inclusive resorts, intending to hold and operate them for decades, as a legitimate business. In other countries, they prefer to buy or build houses, because those countries allow limited-liability corporations owned by shell companies to buy and sell houses. And that includes Panama. Almost a hundred percent of non-government land in Panama is owned by limited-liability corporations, and we simply have no idea if the real owners are legitimate Panamanians or foreigners or Colombian cartels."

That was true, Dan thought. A quirk of Latina culture was that one never showed one's wealth. So any item of value, be it a car or house, was always purchased through a *Sociedad Anónima*, or SA, which operated as a limited-liability corporation and, more importantly, as a social cloak that eased the inequality of wealth between neighbors. Everyone always said they were "just renting" even if they owned their house.

"I'm sorry for being so long-winded," James said, "but I wanted you to understand why we started investigating the Panama money trail, but I'll try to get to the point now. We've known for many years through our confidential sources that a certain bank in Colombia was accepting large deposits of cash from one of the newer cartels known as El Cuadrante. The Cuadrante cartel was a splinter group that arose in

Medellín after the Cali cartel was broken up in 1995…”

“Cuadrante?” Dan interrupted.

“Yes,” James said. “Evidently named after a neighborhood of Medellín known as the Quadrant.”

Don Fernando leaned forward. “Excuse me,” he said, “but *cuadrante* is also a colombiano slang word for *dial*… as in a clock face.”

Dan looked at don Fernando and tried to absorb that new information.

“Really?” said James. “I didn’t know that.” He jotted that down in his notebook and then continued. “Anyway, the Cuadrante cartel was both depositing and withdrawing large amounts of cash from this particular bank. Now, a bank in Colombia accepting large cash deposits is nothing new, but what caught our attention was that when this cartel went to withdraw the cash, they only wanted brand new bills. This is usually done when a criminal gang wants to move money across a border—they want clean bills because most drug money literally smells like drugs. Almost all the US dollars deposited in Colombian banks have traces of cocaine and other drugs on the bills themselves because they come from drug dealers in the states who are always handling drugs and even using the rolled up money to snort drugs. So when the cartel wants to move large sums of money, for example, across the US border, they want brand new bills that won’t alert the drug-sniffing dogs at the border. So we figured that when the Cuadrante cartel started demanding brand new US dollars from this Colombian bank, they were going to be moving that cash into Panama—because they didn’t want to be stopped at the border by drug-sniffing dogs, and because Panama accepts US dollars without question. Normally, US dollars move south to Colombia, but here we believed the dollars were being shipped north into Panama, and we wanted to find out why. We wanted to follow the money.

“And how to do this? Well, the Colombian bank had to buy their new US dollars from the US Treasury. So we asked the Treasury to print special bills with a second magnetic strip embedded on the side so we could track the money. This magnetic strip can be quickly read by a handheld electronic reader we use—you could put one of these marked bills in a stack of a thousand regular bills, and our reader would detect it. It's a much faster system than checking individual serial numbers. So the Treasury simply sold these new bills to this Colombian bank, and we just followed the money. The bills, as I told Dr. Vargas, are legitimate... they're just marked. We arranged periodic courtesy trainings and inspections at all the Panamanian banks and discretely scanned their cash, so we knew which banks those bills were eventually deposited in, and then we could drill down and try and identify who was depositing them... and in every case, it was condominium construction companies. And it was happening all over Panama. We estimate that seventy-five percent of all new condominium construction in the past five years has been funded by these marked bills."

Jorge Manuel suddenly blurted out, "Are you going to arrest them?

James pursed his lips. "No," he said. The only crime they've committed in Panama was that the driver entered the country without declaring money in excess of $10,000. And to speak frankly, we can't even stop the drugs coming into Panama, much less this cash. No, at this point we are simply gathering evidence."

Then Dan spoke: "But you're telling us this now because somehow the secret of the magnetic strip has gotten out."

James raised one eyebrow, and nodded his head. "Yes, exactly."

Dan's mind was racing. "So these two girls may have been killed simply to get marked money back from them?"

"I don't know that," James said. "We know that somehow the bank in Colombia figured out the money was different, and they told the cartel. How these people here," James said, pointing to the chart on the blackboard, "how they found out about it—*if* they found out about it—we just don't know."

Jorge Manuel spoke up again. "But can't you arrest the construction companies?"

"No," James said, "First of all, we don't know who owns them, who controls them. What we're trying to do is to unravel the chain of shell companies that have deposited this money in the Panamanian banks... but it's like those wooden Russian nesting dolls—each shell company is owned by another one, and we have no jurisdiction against them anyway. We're simply gathering evidence that we can hand over to our government so that, at some higher-up level, government leaders might negotiate ways to stop this money laundering."

"Why would they?" Dan asked. "Money is rolling in, providing jobs, and boosting the economy. Why would any Latin American country want to stop that?"

James shrugged, and said, "That's above my level."

Don Fernando spoke up for the first time. "And in the meantime, our country will be totally owned by colombianos."

"Look," James said, "Nobody wants to stop the cartels more than the United States. It's our children who are being hooked on these drugs. But until there is transparency in the ownership of property and the movement of money, there's very little we can do except to keep looking for patterns and gathering evidence. We try to focus on key players when we can identify them and take them out of circulation, but we know that every time we break up one cartel, another one appears."

Dan's head began to hurt, but he forced himself to stay focused. "Getting back to this case," Dan said. "I have a couple of questions."

"Please," James said.

"Number one, do you know who this Hernán person is?"

"No," said James.

"Nor the identity of this enforcer that this cartel sent to find Hernán?"

"No."

"How about this tattoo of a faceless clock? Have you ever heard of that before? Is it related to this cartel?" Dan asked

"I have no information on that, but I will ask when I get back to Washington."

Dan frowned, then asked, "Were there condominium companies here in La Chorrera that deposited some of this marked money?"

"Yes, quite a few."

"All in one bank?"

"No," James answered. "The deposits were all in different banks. We don't have any indication that any of the banks in this city knew about the money laundering. Someone would sell a tract of land and deposit marked money. A company would come to town with a contract to build a condominium and open an account with marked money. Or workers might get paid in marked money every week and deposit some of their money. There was no pattern to it."

"But you have a list of the condominiums involved and maybe a list of who their agents or managers are here in town?" Dan asked.

"Yes."

"Can we get a copy of that list?" Dan asked.

James hesitated. He seemed to think for a minute, then finally said, "Yes, you can. I will prepare one before I leave."

"Can we also get one of those hand-held detectors, so that we can identify this money?" Dan asked.

"I would have to get authorization for that, but I believe you can. We are going to stop using that particular marking strip because it's been discovered, so I don't see why you couldn't have one of the detectors."

Dan hesitated on the next question, but then asked,

"Do you see any stopping or slowing down of this process? That is, do you have any reason to believe that the cartels will stop buying Panamanian land as a way of laundering money?"

James sighed, and said, "No, I don't think it will diminish. If anything, it will only escalate."

Dan rubbed his forehead. His head was really throbbing now. He looked up at the group and asked, "Does anyone else have any other questions?"

"I just have one, Dani," don Fernando said, and then turning to James he asked, "And you say that this is happening all over Panama, not just in La Chorrera?"

"In terms of Colombian drug cartels," James answered, "it's happening all over Panama, Costa Rica, the Dominican Republic, Belize, and Ecuador—anywhere that the cartels think they can build something that they can sell, down the road, to retirees, investors, or tourists. And of course it's a world-wide phenomenon, but that money comes from sources other than Colombia. It continues in the United States and Europe, for example, except that laundered money is coming from China, Russia, and the Middle East. It is the new money laundering model."

There was a long silence in the room. Finally, Dan asked quietly, "How long are you in town?"

"I fly out tomorrow night," James replied. I'm staying at the Marriot here in La Chorrera. I'll leave you my card in case you have any questions."

Chapter Thirty-Five

Dan sat silent on the ride back to Villa Rosario. Vicente and don Fernando were discussing everything that Agent Dixon had said, but Dan was wrapped up in his own thoughts. Conducting that meeting had exhausted him. Normally he could turn his cop brain on for short periods of time, but this meeting had lasted for almost two hours. His head was pounding, and his body felt as if it had been run over by a truck. He had forgotten how much he hated playing the role of the in-charge detective, the totally emotionless analytical anti-crime cop. He wasn't a cop any more. He didn't want to be that way, to act that way, to think that way, to talk that way. He had left that world more than ten years ago for good reason—it had been killing him, slowly squeezing the life out of him. He had had no choice but to leave Los Angeles if he wanted to survive, if he wanted to feel human again.

Dan also realized why his head was hurting—because what he really wanted to do was cry—cry and wail and scream and grieve... Why couldn't he do that? It was bad enough that he hadn't been able to let himself fall completely in love with Magali when he had the chance, but he couldn't even let himself grieve for her—for her and for himself—now that she was gone. How fucked up was he? And he wanted to lash out, too—lash out against the world; against men who thought they owned the sex workers whose time they paid for; against drug dealers who valued money over human life; against cartels; against all those Americans whose appetite for drugs subsidized the cartels; against lawyers who made money laundering possible; against governments for being so impotent against organized crime; and against the FBI for marking money in such a detectable way that the Colombian bank discovered it. Who knew what random combination of events had lined up in such a way to snuff out Magali's life? Dan didn't know, so he blamed the world.

Meanwhile, Vicente was saying to don Fernando: "So maybe this Hernán fellow was not a renegade from the cartel after all, Capitán. Maybe he was part of this cartel, and that's why he had that tattoo. Maybe they were stealing from another cartel."

Don Fernando glanced over at Dan. He could tell that Dan did not want to join the conversation.

"I don't know, Vicente," don Fernando said. "And we may never know. But I also don't think it matters. These men did evil things, and you see how death caught up with them."

"Yes, Capitán," Vicente said. "But only with the foot soldiers. Their bosses remain free to do continue doing bad things. We don't even know who they are."

"Not yet, Vicente, not yet. But my experience is that justice always catches up with everyone—either death or justice—but no one can escape either one."

Vicente sighed. "I hope that is true, Capitán," he said. "But sometimes it seems that evil always wins."

Dan had not been listening to their conversation, but somehow Vicente's last words found their way into Dan's ears, and when Dan heard them, he couldn't help himself. He started to cry.

Chapter Thirty-Six

Three weeks passed. As a detective in Los Angeles, it had been Dan's practice never to divulge the details of a case to anyone outside of the investigation of that case—and this habit was still strong. But Dan felt that Ricardo had a right to know the whole truth about Magali's death—or to be more accurate, the paltry collection of facts that constituted everything Dan knew about her death. But Dan didn't know how to explain to Ricardo his history and use of ayahuasca, nor how to explain his meetings with Magali's ghost, so he decided to omit those parts. He wouldn't have minded if Ricardo knew, but he simply didn't know how to tell him about those things.

And so it was that on this particular Tuesday evening, Dan and Ricardo were sitting at a small table in El Balcón, a quiet bar and restaurant in Villa Rosario. Ricardo was drinking wine. Dan was drinking whiskey.

Dan had just finished summarizing everything for Ricardo that he had told James Dixon, what James Dixon had shared at that meeting, and the fact that there had been no developments in the case for the last three weeks.

"Nothing?" was Ricardo's response.

"No, nothing," Dan said. "The Colombian National Police Laboratory never got back to Dr. Vargas; we haven't heard anything more from the FBI; Vicente's fingerprint collection from Rosa's house hasn't yielded any suspects; and we have no idea where Hernán's body is... although you know how it is in the Panama jungle—bodies decompose so fast. I doubt we'll ever find it."

"And the person who shot them all?" Ricardo asked.

"Just faded back across the border," Dan said.

"What about the condominium companies?"

"Well, don Fernando and Jorge Manuel are still working that list. Of course, they are all SA's, so we have no idea who the actual owners are. Personally, I doubt they'll find out anything."

"Jeez Louise, Dan!" Ricardo exclaimed. He sat there quiet for a minute, thinking about everything Dan had shared. Finally he said, "Well, at least there are no more of these scopolamine murders... at least the murderers are gone."

"Yeah," Dan said. "That may be the only consolation. But it just eats away at me that we just don't know exactly what happened; that there's no one to hold accountable; that Magali's death was so pointless... and so mysterious. I know it wouldn't change anything if I knew exactly what really happened, but somehow—I don't know, but—somehow if I knew what really happened and why it happened, I think I could accept it more."

Ricardo nodded his head, thought for a moment, and then said, "You know, when I lived back in the States, I knew this doctor. He was a friend of mine. And he was a good doctor, a good guy. And he had this patient who had been coming to see him ever since he was a young man. And this patient was a decent guy too, and in good health. And you know how it is with doctors and patients—after a number of years, of decades, they develop a solid relationship. After all, you tell your doctor everything. Anyway, at some point, this patient came down with some kind of illness, so he went to see this doctor, and the doctor did the usual tests, but everything came back negative. But the guy kept getting sicker. So the doctor started doing more tests, trying to figure out what was wrong with the guy. Then he brought in a consultant. But they still didn't know. And they were treating him with antibiotics and stuff, just shooting in the dark, trying to cure him. But he kept getting sicker and sicker. So finally they sent him to the Mayo Clinic. This guy had money, so expense wasn't an issue. And he stayed there for a week, and they did every test in the world on this guy. But no dice. And it made no sense. The guy wasn't that old. He had been in good health. He had exercised regularly, ate sensibly. There were no weird family diseases, no genetic diseases. But they just couldn't figure out what was killing him... And finally, he died. All the money in the world couldn't discover the diagnosis or save him. And my friend, the doctor, was really devastated by this. Not only had he lost a friend, but the guy's death shook my friend's faith in medicine, almost destroyed his conviction that with enough patience and testing and medical knowledge, he could save someone from dying. He almost quit being a doctor."

Dan was listening carefully. "What eventually happened to him?"

"He went on, like we all do. He got through it, somehow, and resumed his practice. I think it humbled him, maybe scared him, maybe made him realize how little we know, and how short our time is."

Dan nodded. "Yeah," was all he could say.

"I mean, what else can we do," Ricardo asked, "except to go on? Magali was special—we both know that—but our lives don't stop. We go on for some reason, or maybe for no reason, but we go on until we stop. I don't know if there's an afterlife or not—if consciousness continues up there in some void—but if there is... if Magali thinks of us, you know that she would want us to go on."

The image of that infinite river of souls spiraling down to the center of the earth that Dan had seen at Magali's last visit flashed through Dan's mind. He didn't know what to say to Ricardo at that moment. He knew Magali no longer existed—that the consciousness that had allowed her to stay in Villa Rosario as a ghost for those few days after her death was certainly gone—pulverized, evaporated, and assimilated into the consciousness of millions upon millions of other dead souls. Magali simply wasn't here anymore. Dan accepted that. Neither God nor ayahuasca could bring her back.

But he also remembered what she had said about not missing this life because it was too "thin", and Dan did not accept that—he didn't believe life was thin. His memories of Magali were rich and detailed. Every time he sat on his balcony and drank coffee and stared out over the central valley in the distance beyond Villa Rosario, he marveled at how rich life was. Even sitting at this table with his old friend Ricardo, talking quietly about the death of a mutual lover had its own rich tapestry of memory and meaning.

Finally, Dan said, "Yeah, you're right. She would have wanted us to go on."

Chapter Thirty-Seven

It was almost midnight. Father Lopez had felt tired most of the day. But as evening had come on, he wasn't sleepy. Perhaps the wine was giving him energy, he thought wistfully. Wine was such a wonderful invention, he mused. Or was it a discovery? He thought about this for a moment as he sipped at his glass. Ancient people—probably monks, he thought—discovered that when grape juice spoiled, it fermented. But someone had to invent the process for making wine on a large scale. Probably monks, he again thought. Monks not only had the time to develop the process, but the motivation. For who needed wine more than monks? No one, he thought, and smiled. Monks, and priests... and nuns!—Father Lopez had known many nuns who kept a bottle of wine in their closets hidden under their scratchy sackcloth undergarments. Yes, the Church needed wine, and thus the Church should receive the credit for the invention of wine... No wait, he thought: maybe *development* is the better word. The monks developed the process for making wine. Yes, he decided, wine had been developed, not discovered or invented. Developed was the best word.

Having resolved that issue, he reached over to the small table by his large chair where the bottle of wine was sitting, and he poured a little into his glass. Just half a glass more, he told himself, before he went to bed.

Such a pleasant evening, he thought. The day had been hot, but the night had brought a cool breeze, and he wouldn't need the fan to sleep tonight. In fact, he might even need a light blanket. It was a nice time of year.

His thoughts drifted about, remembering different people, thinking about his congregations, all the tragedies, the few triumphs, the years arranging funding to repair the Church, the politics of Church life, the fights with the Archdiocese over various issues that they had no business sticking their noses into, the various outcomes... all the people... all of their faces.

But the wine was blurring all the edges of all the faces. It was a very pleasant feeling. Even Magali's face blurred into the crowd, along with Jenny's, and her husband Ted, and even his friend don Fernando.

He made a mental note to have lunch soon with don Fernando. It was enjoyable to share a meal and discuss the old times. Just lunch, though. He didn't need to drink at lunch. Dinner time, however, was reserved as his own quiet time in his cottage, for just a simple meal and wine. But lunch with don Fernando would be nice. They had been friends for so many decades...so many long decades...

He looked at his glass. Just one sip left. Okay. Blood of the lamb. Thank you God, for making wine.

He finished the glass and placed it on the table next to the bottle. "I'll wash them tomorrow," he said to himself. Then he got up slowly and made his way over to the bed.

But he ran his tongue over his teeth. "I should brush my teeth," he told himself. "No sense in letting them get all wine-stained. What would my congregation think?" So he carefully made his way into the bathroom, brushed his teeth, used the toilet, and then made his way back to the bed.

He sat on the edge of the bed, kicked off his slippers, and then stood up and undid his white cotton pants and hung them over the chair by the bed, then slipped off his shirt and placed that over his pants. He kept his undershorts on, and slipped into bed, pulling the sheet up over him. He lay there for a minute, then sat up and reached down to the foot of the bed and unfolded the thin blanket that was there and spread that over the sheet, and lay back down. Yes, that was perfect.

He lay there for a while, letting his thoughts drift. He began to fall asleep. His thoughts were drifting. And soon he was asleep.

And then, sometime during the night, Father Lopez simply died.

Chapter Thirty-Eight

Now, I can tell you, dear Reader, that not all souls linger in this world like Magali's did. Some souls pass directly into the earth without consciousness. And so it was with Father Lopez's soul. It simply left his body and descended right into the center of the world, without pain, without suffering, and without consciousness. I don't know why it is that some people suffer and others don't, why some people die young, and others molt away slowly. It's just the way it is.

Nor can I explain why there is evil. In some ways, Vicente was right—evil always seems to triumph. But certainly Dan is right, too—that life is rich and full of memory and meaning. It is rich and full of meaning despite the fact that we really never know the full truth about why things happen the way they do. The only thing I *can* tell you is that people seem to continue to do the same things they've always done, until something interrupts them.

And of course, Death is the final interruption, the uninvited guest. And it comes to all of us. It will come to me, and it will certainly come to you. When it comes for us, it is an earthquake that swallows us whole. And when it comes to people that we love, it is a tremor that shakes us, that frightens us, that stops us and makes us think. It makes us think of who we love, why we love, where we have failed in love, and most of all, how short life is.

And so, I share my little stories of Villa Rosario for that reason. These are the people I love, some of whom I have loved for a long long time, and some of whom I have failed to love. And I share these stories mostly because, for all of us, life is short... all too short. Try to love. It's really all we can do.

-FIN-

ABOUT THE AUTHOR

Over the past thirty years, Robert Rahula has published dozens books of prose and poetry in Spain and in the United States. While he remains relatively undiscovered in the United States, he is revered in Spain as the founder of the "portilla" style of popular Spanish poetry: non-metered fluid verse that deals with love, loss, bisexuality, separateness, and growing older.

Robert was born in Spain to an American father and Spanish mother, but grew up in Virginia on the farm of his paternal grandparents. He returned to Menorca, Spain, in the 1960s to pursue his writing career. These days he travels in Europe, Central and South America for several months a year, giving readings and lectures, and spends the rest of his time writing, dividing his time between Spain and the United States.

All of Robert's English books are available through Amazon Kindle, including his groundbreaking erotic novel *Messieurs*; his second English novel *Panamaniac*; his erotic murder mystery *Island of Misfits*; his surreal novel *Day Another Paradise In*; his acclaimed supernatural novel *One Last Fling*; his "sexistential" novel *Conversations in a Belgian Bar*; as well as his other "Dan Landes Mystery" novels: *Bathhouse Stories*, *All the Yage in Reno*, and *Exigent Circumstances*.

Seven volumes of Robert's English poetry are also available on Amazon: *Trigger Points*; *Inside the Locked Heart*; *Camino*; *Migration*; *I Sing the Body Politic*; *Wonderland*; *From Whose Bourn*; an anthology of his English poems and short stories, *Half-Life*; and a collection of his most famous Spanish poems, *Poemas Españoles*. Other poems, along with his blog on writing and his tour itinerary, appear on his Facebook page and on his website robertrahula.com.